Venomous Dunes

Arla Jones

Acknowledgements

I would like to thank my editor Kate Seger for the awesome work and also my illustrator Dom Sabasti for the beautiful images, and TMT Cover Designs for the cover.

Dedication

I would like to thank my family for being there for me.

Contents

The Lost Tomb

Chapter 1

Hotel Alhambra, 1940

"It's Christmas Eve, and your sister is cooped up inside her hotel room. What on earth did she do this time?" Sawyer grumbled, sitting in the bar with Lillian's brother Jack Stiller.

Sawyer had flown them from the Alps to Cairo without any trouble. After landing, they had taken two rooms at

Hotel Alhambra, where Jack had found Sawyer the last time.

The bartender was the same carrot top who had served Sawyer before he left with Jack for the cursed expedition in Germany with Dina, mummies, and the Nazis. The bartender was not a young man; he had deep lines on his cheeks and forehead and a large potbelly covered by a white shirt and black pants.

A minty smell lingered in the air. Many visitors like the mint-flavored drinks and tea, and the hotel's manager had instructed his employees to use the mint scent to make the customers feel welcome.

Jack and Sawyer had chosen to hang in the bar instead of sitting in the lobby in the wicker chairs and tables.

"We should do something fancier than drink in the bar," Sawyer complained, pushing the curl of his hair from his forehead. "We could have a Christmas dinner together if you can persuade the bookworm sister of yours to join us."

"If you think you can find a Christmas dinner some-where in this city, then I'm sure I can get Lillian to leave her books, notes, and memoirs for a couple of hours," Jack replied, smiling. He raised his glass, "To us. We saved the world and got rid of the demon Dina. Cheers!"

"Cheers," Sawyer replied and clinked his glass with Jack's. He wore a white long-sleeve shirt, a black belt with a holster, and long black boots, the same ones he had stolen from the SS officer at Berlin airport. He had decided to keep them as they were of good quality. He also kept a Luger in his holster, which he had snatched from one of the dead soldiers near the camp where they had been imprisoned.

A strand of Sawyer's brown hair hung on his forehead while the rest was greased to keep it in style. Jack's hair was ink-black like his sister's, kept short and neat.

"I'll go and check up on Lillian. You think about the dinner plans while I'm gone," Jack said, putting his glass on the counter and standing up. He returned to the floor where they had their rooms. His was next to Lillian's, and Sawyer's room was on the other side.

Jack knocked on Lillian's door, then tried the doorknob, and it opened. "Lillian! Are you here? Your door was unlocked."

"Yes, I'm here. I was just about to come and find you," Lillian replied, emerging from the bathroom. She was all dolled up: her dark hair was curled and reached her shoulders, and she wore a red dress that revealed her curvy figure.

Jack looked at her and said, "I came here to ask you to join us for dinner. It's Christmas Eve. We should do something fun."

"I agree. That's why I got dressed. What do you think about this one? I went shopping earlier and found it," Lillian said and twirled around, and the hem of the dress blew up around her revealing her well-shaped, tanned legs and high-heel shoes.

Jack squinted. "Do you plan to seduce someone? You know I'm your brother, and I will keep away anyone who even looks at you suspiciously or talks to you inappropriately."

Lillian laughed happily. "I know that. I'm just happy to be alive and have two handsome men to take me to dinner. Let's go!" She grabbed Jack by the arm, and they walked down the hallway and found Sawyer waiting for them at the bar.

When Jack saw Lillian, he whistled. "Captain Sawyer at your service, ma'am!"

Lillian blushed, and her cheerful laugh echoed in the bar. "Captain Sawyer! Can't we finally use first names? We've been together in dangerous situations, and I think I deserve to know your first name."

"It's Roy. Roy Sawyer at your service, Lillian." Roy Sawyer took her hand and kissed it. There was more to the kiss than a platonic gesture, and they both knew it. Lillian's eyes widened, and her mouth opened in a silent sigh. Sawyer kept her tiny hand in his callused one for a bit longer than necessary.

Jack assessed the situation, and he had a feeling he was the third wheel in the group. He pushed his hands into his pocket. *I hope Sawyer is a good guy and does not plan to se-*

duce my sister because I will kill him if he does that, regard-

less of our past adventure together, Jack thought grumpily.

Chapter 2

Lillian, Jack, and Sawyer

"Where do we go for dinner? I would like to have some traditional Christmas food instead of rice and kebab," Lillian said, walking with Jack and Sawyer outside. It was balmy weather, the stars were up in the indigo-blue sky, and the moon was almost full.

"I have a surprise for you two," Sawyer replied, grinning. "I know a few Englishmen here, and they have organized an old-fashioned Christmas party down by the British Embassy. The Americans will be joining them too. That's how they got enough booze and food to serve everyone. The only thing they don't have is a Christmas tree, but I think they have figured out how to decorate a palm tree."

"That sounds great," Lillian replied walking slowly and a bit wobbly in her new high-heel shoes. All their clothes were in the trunk of the vehicle, which was lost somewhere at the airport when they embarked on the blimp. She had hoped she would find their luggage somewhere, but that was probably not likely with the war going on.

She had bought some clothes when they arrived in Cairo with the money wired to them from London's bank. Jack had bought a couple of pairs of shirts and trousers.

Mostly Lillian wished she could have taken all the books from the deserted excavation camps. So many books were left there because Dina had killed the other archeologists. She would have enjoyed reading those volumes and remembered many she had not even seen before. *Perhaps, we could go back to get the books*, she wondered and glanced at Jack and Sawyer. Would they go with her, or would they tell her that she was crazy going back there? Either way, she was going to suggest returning to the excavation area. She wanted to see if anything was left in the tomb or excavation that would be valuable for research.

Jack's thoughts were not on archeology; instead, he thought about Lillian and Roy Sawyer. Was there something going on between the two of them? He tried to analyze if he liked it or not. Sawyer had proved to be a swell guy, but would he be a good husband? That was another question. He was a smuggler and drank too much. He didn't have any means to support Lillian. He introduced himself as a captain. Where did he get the title, or was it only self-promotion?

"Sawyer, why do you call yourself a captain?" Jack decided to ask directly.

Sawyer glanced at him and said slowly, "I was a captain in the French Sixth Foreign Infantry Regiment in Algeria.

I did my time there and left just before this war started," he replied. "I was in the Battle of France until June, then left. I don't want to go back. I saw enough death for the rest of my life. Besides, getting the officer's rank was only because I saved a few soldiers in the battle." He shook his head. "They didn't want to let me go. I had signed a contract to serve five years twice, and it was mandatory to serve the years you signed for. Nobody could stop you if you walked out after your time was up."

"Ten years of service in the Foreign League? That's impressive," Jack said, impressed. He looked at Sawyer with different eyes. He had no idea this smuggler had a distinguished military career behind him.

Chapter 3

On the Way to the Party

Even this late in the evening, the wind gusts are warm. That's Cairo for you, Lillian thought. *Back in London, I would be walking in the rain, battling the bone-chilling wind.*

That evening was special for so many because of the Christian tradition. However, it was different for Germans. The Nazis did not want to encourage the Jewish holidays. That's what Christmas was to them, so they tried to encourage winter solstice celebration instead. However, when other countries celebrated outside Germany, the Germans also decided to have their party. Many soldiers had a night off, and you could hear their loud singing in the bars: Exalted Night, Fatherland, and other party-approved songs.

Cairo had become a congregation of many foreigners and spies of various regimes. However, as Egypt was also an important source of historical artifacts, the damaging fighting and bombing stayed away from the culturally important areas.

Lillian walked between Jack and Sawyer, and the warm wind blew from the desert blowing up the sand and dry dust from the sidewalks on their way to the embassy. The wind hissed ominously as it passed through the narrow alleys and swirled in front of them. Frowning, Lillian stared at the spiraling dust ahead. She remembered the last time she had seen one: with Dina, the demon who had appeared from the cursed tomb and dragged them along to Berlin. She recalled how the swirling sand had appeared under Jack's feet at the archeologist camp, and Dina had tried to sink him into the sandpit. Slowing her pace, Lillian glanced around and sighed in relief No sign of Dina anywhere.

"What's wrong?" Jack asked when he noticed the panicked look in Lillian's eyes.

"The sand swirl reminded me of Dina again," Lillian replied.

"She's gone! She could not have survived the elevator and the explosion," Jack replied, putting his arm over his sister's shoulders.

Sawyer glanced at them. "Don't worry. Dina is back in the underworld. She can't disturb us any longer." He gestured to a white building with bright lights and said, "That's our destination. We'll have a great party tonight. No more mummies, snakes, beetles, or Dina. That's all past."

The moment he said that a swarm of locusts flew out of nowhere and startled her. She screamed and swatted the giant locusts away from her hair and dress. Then all three of them dashed inside the party building. "That's not normal," Lillian said, shaking. "Locusts in December. Something's wrong."

"It was nothing. Forget about it. We are inside now," Sawyer said, brushing away the last locusts. "It must have been a warm season. You know I've seen locusts swarming in February too. It depends on the weather. They can't live and survive in the cold, but it has been humid and hot here this fall." He sounded convincing because he didn't want to believe that the locusts had anything to do with Dina-demon again.

Lillian tilted her head as she looked at the Egyptian locusts. They were large and walking slowly to the side of the hallway. Someone said behind her, "They are harmless to humans, but they destroy crops. We posted an alert on the wall because these locusts can eat the crop in hours." She turned around and saw a distinguished-looking tall man in his forties who extended his hand and said, "Welcome! I'm Ambassador Raymond Hare."

Lillian shook his hand, smiling, and Sawyer introduced the siblings to the ambassador, who said, "I'm pleased to have all of you here. It's a party, and the more people are here, the better."

Chapter 4

At the Christmas Party

Ambassador Raymond Hare remained by the doorway greeting all the incomers while Lillian, Jack, and Sawyer walked along the edge of the room, heading to the tables filled with delicious-looking dishes, including ham, turkey, different casseroles, puddings, cakes, and cookies. The drinks were free in the bar with a scarlet punch and eggnog.

The expansive room exuded festive cheer; its walls adorned with intricately crafted paper-cut snowflakes that glistened in the soft glow of twinkling lights. The centerpiece of the holiday spectacle, a colossal Christmas tree that defied tradition by masquerading as a palm tree bedecked in Yuletide attire, commanded attention from a raised platform. The unconventional arboreal display featured an opulent array of decorations, with paper spirals cascading down like whimsical garlands, and an abundance of tinsel draping its branches. Glass baubles, resplendent with a dazzling sparkle, further obscured the strange Christmas tree beneath.

As if emerging from a magical winter wonderland, the band stage materialized at the back of the room, a bastion of musical enchantment. The elevated platform supporting the festive fir was enveloped in a festive embrace of vibrant red ribbons, adding an extra layer of holiday charm to the already enchanting scene. Amidst the jubilant atmosphere, the amalgamation of unconventional elements created a unique and captivating holiday setting, where the spirit of Christmas intertwined seamlessly with tropical whimsy. The band was dressed as nutcrackers of the ballet Nutcracker: shiny black hats, fake black mustaches, and wearing red uniforms reminding Lillian of King George VI's guards in Buckingham Palace. They played Christmas classics and Big Band dance music like Ain't Misbehavin', Strings of Pearls, and I'll be Seeing You.

In the adjacent room, couples swayed and twirled gracefully across the polished dance floor, their movements synchronized to the rhythmic cadence of music that filled the air with festive energy. The ambiance was one of joy and celebration as the wide glass double doors, standing ajar, invited in the gentle evening breeze. Beyond the threshold, the night sky painted a canvas of stars, casting a soft glow that mingled with the warm, ambient light emanating from the festivities within.

As the dance floor became a stage for shared moments and laughter, the openness of the double doors served as a seamless connection between the revelry indoors and the allure of the world beyond. The subtle interplay of music, laughter, and the occasional rustle of leaves in the breeze created a harmonious symphony, blending the jubilant spirit of the celebration with the tranquility of the outdoor expanse. Lillian took all in as she followed Jack and Sawyer to grab the food on the plate and then the drinks. They found a cozy corner table and sat down to eat. It was lovely to have a normal feeling Christmas party after all the chaos in Berlin with Dina and the Nazis.

While Lillian watched the crowd mingling, laughing, and dancing, she had a surreal feeling that this was not real or that something awful was going to happen.

As Sawyer headed to the bar to fetch a fresh round of drinks, Jack surreptitiously stole a glance at Lillian, only to find her listlessly pushing her food around on her plate. Concern etched on his face, he leaned in and queried, "What's the matter? You haven't touched your food."

Lillian met her brother's gaze, a cloud of unease lingering in her eyes, and confessed, "I don't know, Jack. It's just this lingering sense of foreboding as if something ominous is on the horizon."

Jack's brow furrowed with a mixture of curiosity and worry. "Why do you say that? Is there something you're aware of that I'm not?"

The weight of Lillian's premonition hung in the air, casting a shadow over the otherwise lively ambiance of the surroundings. As the anticipation of an impending revelation loomed, the clinking of glasses and distant hum of conversation provided a stark contrast to the growing tension between the siblings, leaving an unspoken question dangling in the air — a question that held the key to the mysterious undercurrents tugging at the edges of their tranquil evening.

Lillian shook her head. "No, I know it's not anything concrete. I have a feeling that we missed something either in Germany or by the tomb's excavation area. I'd like to go back to see the camps near the tomb. Maybe that will put my mind at ease."

"Okay, we can do that. Eat now. This is free food, and pretty good too," Jack replied, stuffing ham and potatoes in his mouth.

When Sawyer returned with the punch for everyone, Jack said, "Lillian thinks we have overlooked something. She wants to visit Dina's tomb and the excavation area."

Looking worried, Sawyer replied, "Dina is gone. She died. She can't come back, can she?" He remembered Dina's touches and whispers when she told him she would like to have him as her slave and shivered. He didn't want Dina to return to this world again, and if there was anything they had forgotten, they should visit the tomb. "I never visited the archeological excavation area, and I didn't see the tomb where Dina came from. Do you believe there is something evil that could come alive like Dina?"

"I don't know," Lillian replied honestly. "I have a feeling like I have forgotten something important. It's nagging me, and I can't place what it is and why it's important."

Jack leaned back on his chair. "We'll take the jeep and go there tomorrow. No reason to postpone the visit. You can pick up all the books and materials from the abandoned camps, and then we can see about the tomb." He paused and added, "I'm not sure if it is safe to go inside the tomb. Remember, Dina came from it. How do we know there is not more of her kind in there?"

"We may not know for sure, but that uncertainty is precisely why a visit is warranted. I don't want anyone else to stumble upon that cursed tomb and release something like Dina or Dina herself again" Lillian responded, a contemplative expression gracing her features. "I appreciate your understanding of my concerns. Tonight, let's immerse ourselves in the festivities and momentarily set aside these concerns." Casting a fleeting glance toward the band, her eyes caught the subtle promise of distraction in the rhythm of their instruments.

As the musicians transitioned into a melodic and slow-tempo tune, Lillian seized the opportune moment. With a whimsical smile, she turned to the gentlemen and extended an invitation, "Would one of you gallant gentlemen care to share a dance with me? It's Christmas Eve, and

I'm in the mood for a dance—a magical waltz beneath the enchanting glow of holiday lights." The request, layered with the spirit of the season, hung in the air, an invitation to partake in the joyous celebration and momentarily dispel the shadows of uncertainties that loomed in the background. Roy Sawyer got up before Jack even had time to answer and extended his hand to Lillian. "Let's go."

Chapter 5

A Kiss in the Dark

Ambassador Raymond Hare gave a short Christmas welcome greeting when all the guests had enjoyed their dinner. "Please, stay and enjoy our Nutcracker band and sing along with the familiar songs."

While Lillian and Sawyer had danced together, Jack had made friends with Hare's new secretary, a brunette with sparkling green eyes. He had cornered her near the bandstand, and they were discussing something animatedly when Lillian's eyes met her brother's. Jack winked at her and then returned his full charm and attention to the young secretary, who giggled and smiled like Jack was the most wonderful man in the whole world.

With a gentle gesture, Sawyer enveloped Lillian within the crook of his arm, his voice carrying a warm invitation as he proposed, "How about a stroll in the garden? The evening air might offer a refreshing respite."

Smiling in agreement, Lillian responded, "Yes, that sounds lovely. The heat in here is becoming a bit much." Together, they navigated through the vibrant throng of the partygoers toward the beckoning glass double doors that opened into the enchanting backyard garden. As they stepped outside, a transformative scene unfolded before them.

The garden, adorned with a myriad of decorative, colorful paper lanterns, exuded an ethereal ambiance that transcended reality. The gentle glow of the lanterns cast a soft, magical light, creating an otherworldly atmosphere that seemed plucked from the pages of a fairy tale. Lillian, captivated by the surreal beauty, couldn't help but express her awe, remarking, "It's like stepping into an enchanted world. The roses and the various lanterns add such a breathtaking touch to the surroundings."

As they continued their leisurely walk, the fragrant perfume of blooming roses wafted through the air, intertwining with the soft shimmer of lantern light. In this oasis of tranquility, Sawyer and Lillian found themselves immersed in a moment of serenity, a temporary escape from the bustling revelry within. The garden, with its whimsical charm, became their world where no one interrupted them.

Sawyer's response came with a sense of familiarity, "Indeed, I remember. I attended this very party last year, and the ambassador received a cascade of positive comments about the decorations. It appears he's chosen to recreate it again this year."

As they strolled through the adorned venue, Lillian, her curiosity piqued, posed a question to Roy Sawyer, "By the way, how long have you been in Cairo?"

"About two years. I came here when I left the Foreign Legion. I had nowhere to go. Going back to London was not in my plans. I wanted to see the world, and after the Foreign League, no place seemed good enough to stay for a long time, so I moved from one place to another while following the rise of Nazis in Germany, and I realized survival and fighting skills might come in handy soon."

Lillian and Sawyer walked on the narrow gravel path that led to a small, white-painted bench under a large palm tree and sat down. Lillian lifted her face, and Sawyer's eyes met hers. They stared at each other a heartbeat longer, and then Sawyer gently grabbed her chin, leaned forward, and lowered his lips to hers. Their first kiss was soft and slow, a sweet exploration of what could be, and then a dark shadow flew past their heads and shrieked.

Startled by a sudden disturbance, Lillian leaped to her feet, her gaze darting anxiously around the surroundings.

"What was that?" she inquired, her expression etched with a mix of surprise and concern.

Sawyer, rising alongside her, followed the trajectory of her alarmed gaze and identified the culprit responsible for interrupting their tender moment. With a penetrating stare, he observed, "A bat. A rather sizable, black bat at that." A flicker of surprise crossed his features as he pondered the unusual behavior. "It's peculiar. Bats are typically averse to light. Why, then, is this one drawn to the lanterns here?"

"My heart is still pounding! It scared me," Lillian said, raising her hand over her heart. She glimpsed suspiciously at the bat. *Was it really an ordinary bat?* She wondered. *We have encountered so many supernatural things after we arrived in Egypt, so I doubt that this bat is anything but normal.*

"Let's go inside," Sawyer said, grabbing her by the elbow, and they hurried inside.

Sawyer had not told her that he had seen dozens of bats in the trees in the backyard, but it had always been dark or shady, not bright lights. *He suspected something else had lured this creature here, but why now? Why did this bat show up now? Was there something more sinister going on? It seemed that whenever he tried to have a moment with a woman, like today with Lillian, something or someone interrupted. It was like he was cursed!* And then it hit him: *Cursed! Dina the demon! She must be doing this. If she can't have me, then no other woman should,* Sawyer thought grumpily. *Should I mention this to Lillian? Yes, perhaps I should,* he decided.

"Lillian, is it possible that Dina cursed me?" Sawyer asked when they approached the double doors leading inside.

"I don't know. I guess it's possible," Lillian replied and turned to study his face. "Why do you ask?"

"Because ever since meeting Dina and her amorous advancements, I haven't been able to be alone with any other woman. Something or someone always interrupts me," Sawyer said crossly.

Lillian laughed, but when she realized that Sawyer was serious, she replied, "I think we need to go back to where this all started. That's the place for answers. I never had a chance to see the tomb. We only went to the camp, and Dina grabbed us there."

"Let's do it soon. I'll do anything to stop this," Sawyer replied. "I don't want to live like a hermit for the rest of my life."

As they reentered the lively dance hall, a mischievous snicker escaped from Lillian's lips because of what Sawyer had just told her, adding a playful note to the ambiance. Sawyer, catching the sound, cast a sidelong glance her way, his expression a blend of curiosity and amusement. A knowing smile played on his lips, acknowledging the shared moment of light-heartedness between them.

Chapter 6

The Bat

Jack was dancing with the secretary, who was giggling to his jokes when Sawyer and Lillian returned inside. Smiling, Lillian nodded to Jack, turned to Sawyer, tilted her head, and suggested flirtatiously, "You should ask me to dance."

Sawyer flashed a quick smile, pulled her to the dance floor, and soon they were next to Jack and his secretary.

Jack said over the secretary's shoulder. "This is Margarite. She works for the ambassador." Then he introduced his sister and Sawyer to Margarite, who smiled and extended her hand to shake theirs.

"We plan to return to our hotel and have some drinks there when this party ends. Would you like to join us?" Sawyer asked Jack.

"Yes, that's a great idea. What do you think?"

Margarite agreed and leaned closer to Jack.

A sudden dark shadow flew in from the garden and circled the room. Its leathery wings flapped in the air, and its mouth opened in a shriek showing sharp white teeth.

"That bat again!" Sawyer said, crouching lower and covering his head as the bat flew toward his head and almost hit him. Lillian screamed, grabbed Sawyer by the waist, and ducked as the bat's large wings aimed to hit her in the face. The bat's eyes gleamed menacingly as it barely missed her face. She was sure it meant to hit her. The eyes looked more human and calculating than any mammal's eyes should.

Quickly, Lillian nudged Sawyer by his arm and said, "We better leave. That bat is not going to leave us alone." Sawyer nodded and watched as the bat flew by Jack and shrieked next to his ear, making Jack curse and try to slap it with his hand. No such luck. The bat was just above his reach, glaring at Jack with its dark eyes. Jack suddenly shivered as if someone else was watching him through the animal's eyes.

"Let's go," he said to Margarite, and they ran to the doorway where Sawyer was already heading with Lillian.

The enormous bat didn't stop but flew in circles around the room. The band had stopped playing as they were also wary of the bat. The celebratory mood was gone, and the couples snuck out of the room, leaving the party early.

Ambassador Hare tried to calm people down, raising his hands and shouting, "Please, stay still. The bat is just scared of the noise and light. It will leave soon." However, his efforts to restore the previous happy atmosphere were for naught.

Sawyer and Lillian met Jack and Margarite outside. It was a sultry night with bright stars peppering the inky blue sky.

Jack put his hand over Margarite's shoulders and said, "Our hotel is not far away. A short walk that way." He gestured forward to the busy street with pedestrians and cars occupying the street. The merchants of daytime were gone, but the city was still buzzing with restaurant-goers and soldiers looking for Christmas parties. Not much else to do that time of year when the war was ongoing, and you never knew how many days you had to live.

Sawyer recognized German, American, and British uniforms as well as a couple of Foreign Legion officers as they walked by. He nodded to them but did not stay to exchange any words, wanting to keep his status as an independent contractor and impartial. He had acquired a new plane from the German businessmen during their last adventure when escaping from the Berghof of the Bavarian Alps and trying to find their way out of the German-conquered and administrated country.

As they walked towards their hotel, Sawyer asked Lillian, "When are you going to tell your brother we plan to go back to the tomb excavation?"

"I think he already knows," Lillian said, looking pensive. She glanced at Jack, who looked distracted, and she sighed. This was not the best evening to meet a charming girl like Margarite. She couldn't compete with evil spirits like Dina, and whatever curses were hidden in her tomb.

Jack felt Lillian's gaze and looked directly at her. He mouthed one word, "Dina?"

Lillian shrugged her shoulders. She didn't know if the bat was sent by Dina, but it had tried to attack the people involved in her demise.

Jack came closer to Lillian and Sawyer, holding his arm over Margarite's shoulders. He locked his eyes with Sawyer and asked, "What was that bat all about?"

"I don't know. It seemed to be attacking us," Sawyer replied, replaying recent events again in his mind. "First, it was outside in the garden, and then it followed us inside and circled close to our heads there too."

"I saw its eyes. They were human-like and menacing. They were not normal bat eyes," Jack commented, furrowing his brows. He glanced at his secretary making sure she didn't look scared.

She wasn't. Instead, Marguerite listened to Jack and Sawyer with piqued interest. "Who is Dina, and what are you talking about?" The guys didn't answer right away, so Margarite looked from Jack to Sawyer with a puzzled expression.

Lillian sighed. *It's better to tell her the truth*, she thought. *Then Marguerite can decide if she still wants to see Jack.* "Dina was an evil spirit, a demon, you might say. She haunted us some weeks ago. She died or went to the underworld, but Jack and Sawyer think this bat was a sign from her—that she's back or she can somehow monitor us and see what we are doing."

Margarite gave a little laugh and covered her mouth with her hand. "That sounds crazy. There are no demons." When she saw the serious faces before her, she asked, "Are you serious? You're telling me that demons do exist?"

"Let's go to the hotel, and we'll tell you the whole story," Jack said, and they continued their walk.

Chapter 7

Hotel Alhambra

When the couples entered Hotel Alhambra's lobby, a group of German officers and some soldiers had occupied all the tables. They had a radio there playing the latest hits.

No more O'Tannenbaum, Jack thought as he led Margarite towards the bar, and Sawyer followed them, holding hands with Lillian.

When they sat down by the bar, one of the German soldiers heard the radio playing Lili Marlene, a hit song from the previous year, 1939, when it was recorded and started singing along.

"A sweet and sad song of two lovers who promise to wait for each other under the lamp by the barracks," Lillian translated the song while Jack and Sawyer ordered whiskies and Bees Knees for the ladies, which was gin with lemon juice and honey.

Jack glanced back at the Germans, turned to Margarite, and said, "I promised I would tell you about the demon we met." His eyes locked with Lillian sitting next to Margarite, and she nodded. Jack started his story. "We were in Berlin a couple of months ago. The demon spirit we told you about took us there. Dina, that was her name, wanted to find her father's golden heart scarab so that she could rule the world."

Margarite looked like she didn't believe a word of what Jack said, so she turned her head to see Lillian and Jack, but they looked deadly serious, so she asked, "Are you serious? This demon thing was real?"

Jack nodded. "Yes, it was. She was about to kill me a couple of times, but Lillian convinced her to let me live." Jack's eyes went to Sawyer's when he added, "Dina seemed to be infatuated with our friend Sawyer here."

Sawyer's eyes watered as his drink went down the wrong pipe, prompting a coughing fit. He turned away, his face reddening, just as Jack flashed a mischievous grin. Of course, he'd have to rub it in, Sawyer thought, shaking his head. He signaled the bartender for another drink, which arrived promptly.

Meanwhile, as the Germans sang in the background, and Jack told the story of the Lost Tomb and about Dina, Lillian surveyed the lobby and the bar. Everything looked normal, like it had been when they left for the Christmas party. She still had an odd feeling that something was off. And then it happened.

The huge bat flew in, circled the lobby, and flew low past the customers' heads.

Margarite screamed and crouched on her chair while the Germans stopped singing and tried to shoo the bat away with their coats and hands. The creature opened its mouth and showed sharp teeth and circled back to the bar where it flew past the couples sitting there, and they could see the creature's eyes, Dina's eyes.

"No, this is not happening again," Sawyer said when he recognized the human-like eyes. "She died. She can't be back."

The bat kept flying and screeching, avoiding all the shooing German soldiers.

Jack ducked when the bat almost hit his head and said, "Lillian! We must go back to the tomb. This all started there. This must end there."

"I know," Lillian replied, barely avoiding the direct hit on her head from the bat's leathery wing.

"Let's go to my room," Lillian said. "The creature can't follow us there. We can lock the door."

Sawyer and Jack grabbed a couple of bottles with them, then took off, leaving the bat in the lobby with the Germans and running to the stairs leading to their hotel rooms. Lillian opened her door, and they all rushed inside and locked it behind them. "Safe," Lillian said, sighing.

"Only temporarily." Sawyer went to the window and closed it too. "That creature or something else will attack us if we don't find a way to permanently put an end to this." He sat by the window and looked at Lillian, who nodded, then moved his eyes to Jack, who did the same.

Margarite cautiously said, "Jack, I like you and want to help you. If you need anything before you go, then let me know. I'm not joining this scary expedition to the lost tomb."

"Thanks, honey," Jack said, putting his arm over her shoulders. "We'll take care of this problem, then we can spend some time together."

Margarite took a note from the nightstand and wrote something on it. "This is my number at Ambassador Hare's office. Call me if you need anything."

Jack glanced at it. She had given her telephone number and her full name Margarite Gunderson. Jack pulled her closer and kissed her gently. "I will be back. I promise."

Margarite blushed. She blinked a few times, glanced at Sawyer and Lillian, and said, "I'll let you plan your trip to the tomb now. I will see you all later."

She walked to the door, opened it, and closed it behind her. Jack looked like he wanted to go after her, but Lillian put her hand on his arm and said, "She's safer if she is not with us. She made the right choice."

"I know," Jack muttered and sat on the bed. "When do we go? And more importantly, what do you think we will need there?"

"Weapons, explosives to close the tomb forever, and water and food for the trip there and back," Sawyer replied.

"I hope we can close the tomb that easily," Lillian said. "What if the curse won't allow us to use explosives, or what if they fail?"

"Do you have a better suggestion?" Sawyer asked.

"No, I don't," Lillian admitted. "I just feel like we should go to the German archeologist camp first and find out what they knew about the tomb because they were the ones who were there first. We should also check the other camp, the British archeologist. I believe the answer is there in their books or their discoveries."

Jack nodded and glanced at Sawyer, who reluctantly nodded too. "More information was better when fighting against a demon like Dina," Jack said.

"If you don't find anything useful in the camps, then we'll try my method," Sawyer said, folding his arms.

"Yes, of course." Lillian turned her eyes to him and smiled. "Let's celebrate the last hours of Christmas Eve now."

"Great idea!" Jack said and poured whiskey from the bottle into three glasses Lillian placed on the table. They all took a glass in their hands and clinked them. "Merry Christmas!"

Chapter 8

The Next Morning

Early next morning, Jack, Lillian, and Sawyer headed downstairs, where they had a quick breakfast at the hotel's lobby with eggs, bacon, toast with strawberry jam and mint tea for Lillian, and strong espresso cups for both men.

The sun was still low on the horizon as they got ready to start their adventure.

Both men wore long-sleeved shirts and knee-length pants with leather boots. They also had Fedora hats to protect them from the sunshine and scarves in case of a sandstorm. They also took pistols, and Sawyer had some dynamite too. Jack guessed Sawyer had carried the dynamite sticks from Berghof when they blasted the elevator shaft.

Lillian took with her a wide-brimmed straw hat, a comfortable long-sleeved white shirt, and tan pants with sturdy shoes. She also had a leather shoulder bag filled with her diary and her written notes about her previous encounter with Dina, a flashlight, bandages, pens, pencils, a notebook, and a sketch pad for making drawings or copying hieroglyphs. She did not take any encyclopedias or reference books with her because she was sure that the two abandoned camps had plenty of those left behind.

The locals and the grave robbers avoided going near the place where so many had died mysteriously. They would never touch the camps and the tents' contents after the carnage that happened there. All the natives feared the killing curse. Lillian was sure she would find the camps in the same state she saw them the last time, except for the weather damage. She still hoped she would find the books and the archeologists' notes, papyri, and whatever else they had found in the excavation area near the tomb before they opened it. She took no shovels, knives, or other tools because she remembered seeing plenty of those when they drove by the area last time.

They took Jack's new jeep, which he had purchased after they returned from their escapades in Berlin and Bavarian Alps. Lillian sat in the backseat while Jack drove and Sawyer gave instructions on which way to drive through the narrow and winding streets and alleys of Cairo without hitting the market squares or German patrols.

Heinrich Himmler, the formidable Reichsführer of the Schutzstaffel and a prominent figure in the Nazi Party, wielded significant power and harbored an intense fascination for the supernatural and occult. This captivating intrigue stemmed from a complex fusion of personal beliefs, esoteric ideologies, and a skewed interpretation of history. Immersed in esoteric and mystic practices, Himmler sought elusive knowledge and ancient wisdom, viewing the occult not merely as a political strategy but as a genuine conviction that supernatural forces could empower the Aryan master race and ensure victory in the war.

Driven by this fervor, Himmler fervently believed that tapping into supernatural or paranormal elements could furnish the Nazi regime with a distinct military advantage. This ambitious pursuit encompassed the quest for mythical artifacts, engagement in occult rituals, and the relentless pursuit of ancient knowledge, all envisioned to bolster the invincibility of the Nazi military. Moreover, Himmler sought to reshape history, intertwining historical events with supernatural elements to validate the actions of the regime.

In his endeavor to instill a sense of mysticism and awe, Himmler incorporated occult rituals and symbols into the practices of the Nazi Party. This calculated move aimed to cultivate an exclusive aura around the party's elite and exert control over the ideology and loyalty of its followers, fostering a sense of exclusivity among the devoted ranks.

Against this backdrop, Lillian, Jack, and Sawyer unwittingly found themselves entangled in the web of Himmler's interests. Unbeknownst to the trio, their previous adventures in Berlin had made them known to this powerful figure. Himmler had decided to keep an eye on the trio and their next moves. In the labyrinthine streets of Cairo, every step taken by the trio was surveilled by the watchful eye of Himmler's spies. Sawyer, well-versed in the meticulous nature of the German officers, anticipated this as they ventured from the confines of their hotel toward the desert in the early morning hours when not many people were awake.

Jack drove through the city, avoiding any German patrols. Sawyer kept his eyes on the traffic behind them, watching out for spies.

Lillian's mind was busy with the tomb and what she should look for there and in the camps. She remembered the first time when she met Dina in the British camp. Dina had taken the body of Lewis Llewellyn, a young archeologist working for the British Museum. Back then, Lillian could not believe that Dina had killed everyone with her powers. She knew that if the Germans could figure out a way to duplicate Dina's powers and transfer them to a living person, they would do it without hesitation. With a supernatural power like that, the Germans would rule the world.

Chapter 9

The Excavation Area

As Jack, Lillian, and Sawyer approached the excavation site containing the long-lost tomb of Dina, the daughter of high priest Thutmose, their anticipation quickly turned to disbelief. Instead of encountering an abandoned locale, they were met with a bustling scene of activity. German soldiers, clad in light brown uniforms, worked tirelessly alongside local hires, transforming the once-desolate area into a hive of excavation, clearing away the remnants of previous workers and archaeologists who had met untimely ends.

Jack, abruptly braking the jeep on the dunes at a distance, allowed them a vantage point to observe the unexpected turn of events. Gazing at the unfolding scene, the trio beheld the meticulous efforts of the German soldiers, their actions betraying weeks of occupation and intense excavation around the tomb's entrance.

The revelation struck a chord with Lillian, prompting her to connect the dots from their past encounters. "I should have guessed this would happen," she admitted slowly, turning the attention of the two men towards her. Recognizing their puzzled expressions, she elucidated, "When Dina compelled us to search for Thutmose's tomb, we discovered it on the opposite side of the pharaoh's graves. His burial site in the Tombs of Nobles had been pilfered, and the tomb, stripped of treasures, pots, and statues, bore the unmistakable mark of German intervention. We followed the trail to Berlin, where we confronted Heinrich Himmler. He sought to harness Dina's powers, yet we thwarted his attempts, ensuring he never met her – except for those unfortunate officers inside Hindenburg and at the airport."

Interrupting the recollection, Jack queried, "We are aware of that. Why do you believe they would find this tomb and commence excavation?"

"Of course, they would," Lillian affirmed. "Himmler is relentless in his pursuit of supernatural power to tip the scales of war in their favor. He knows this is a place where such powers were unearthed – Dina's tomb."

Sawyer, scrutinizing the site, pondered, "Himmler knew the location?"

"Yes, because Walther Wolfe, the chief German archaeologist, had been working alongside the Tombs of the Nobles, under orders from Himmler. Wolfe's frequent progress reports in Egypt indicated his primary task was to uncover anything paranormal or supernatural to aid the German war effort," Lillian explained.

As the trio surveyed the area, Sawyer remarked, "Based on the reports, Himmler dispatched this group to continue the excavation."

Lillian nodded in agreement; her gaze focused on the tomb. "Indeed, and it appears they're not merely clearing the area. I suspect they are searching for something specific."

"What could that be?" Jack inquired, turning to Lillian for insight.

"They might be searching for the books!" Lillian said quietly. "I should have thought about that before."

"Books? What books?" Sawyer furrowed his brows, seeking clarification.

Lillian shook her head, her expression grave. "I hope I'm wrong, but I fear I'm correct. When the Germans raided the high priest's tomb, they failed to locate his scepter, the Black Book of Anubis, and the Golden Book of Ra – powerful artifacts containing ancient spells and curses. I fear they are seeking those very items now."

Jack, brushing his hair with his hand, sought confirmation, "You believe they are searching for the books and the scepter?"

"Yes, I do. Himmler knew where the Black Book was used, and this was the place where Thutmose invoked Anubis to save his daughter Dina. The curse laid by Anubis would ensure Dina's return when the tomb was opened," Lillian replied.

Worry etched across Jack's face, he pressed, "Do you believe the books and the scepter are inside?"

"I don't know, but I wanted this tomb to remain closed and buried. I don't want another encounter with Dina, and I certainly don't want these powerful artifacts in German hands. We must find them first and safeguard them from the Germans and assure our world is safe," Lillian said with conviction.

Sawyer, skeptical about the existence of such objects, voiced his doubt. "These artifacts are part of ancient Egyptian folklore. We can't be sure they even exist in the real world."

"Perhaps, but we cannot be certain," Lillian reasoned.

Jack added a cautious perspective, "If the scepter was solid gold, it might have been stolen by grave robbers. That item might be lost forever."

Lillian, resolute, countered, "We don't know that for sure. We can't afford to take that risk."

As the trio grappled with the uncertainty, Jack questioned their course of action, "So, what's the plan? Confront the Germans and ask them to cease excavation. They won't comply."

"I'm not sure yet. The bat sightings were a sign, a warning that we needed to hasten here. It's as if the bat was trying to alert us," Lillian mused.

"The bat! Do you think it was Dina?" Sawyer, apprehensive, shivered at the thought of encountering Dina once again.

"Perhaps, or it could be another spirit from the underworld signaling that ancient secrets are in peril, urging someone to intervene," Lillian speculated. "We need to act, urgently. I don't want the Germans to wield ancient supernatural powers and demons to win this war. It's morally unjust."

Jack, sensing the gravity of the situation, questioned, "Any idea where to start searching for the books and the scepter?"

"I want to revisit the old camps. I saw some intriguing documents and books there," Lillian suggested, turning to face Jack. "Can we go there and check if the camps are still intact?"

"Sure," Jack acknowledged, starting the jeep as they veered away from the excavation area, setting course for the old camps in pursuit of answers.

Chapter 10

What Next?

"Did you see the uniforms of the soldiers back there?" Jack asked, driving away and then turning towards the old camp area.

"Yes, the ones watching over the work wore the Schutzstaffel's black uniforms, whereas the ones guarding the site sported the olive cotton tropical, which is common for German Afrikakorps," Sawyer replied. "It makes sense if Himmler has ordered this. He has sent his officers to supervise the site. Reichsführer Himmler does not want anyone to reach inside the tomb and find whatever treasure or power he believes exists inside it." His vigilant eyes scanned the dunes glancing backward, ensuring no soldiers had seen or were coming after them.

Jack agreed. "Yes, you're right. Himmler would like to be the one presenting the discovery of any supernatural or paranormal power to Führer und Reichskanzler Hitler himself."

It had been fairly calm all morning with a warm breeze now and then, but as they drove towards the old camps, the wind speed increased, and Lillian pulled her hat tighter on her head. Her long curls flew over her face. She worried that they would end up in the middle of the sandstorm. Checking the horizon, she didn't see a threatening dust storm, so she relaxed.

The next question in Lillian's mind was, why the wind blew harder the closer they got to the archeologists' camps? Was there something that Dina or whoever was haunting them did not want them to find, or did that spirit want them to be the ones to find it? Lillian wasn't sure if the bat had been a friendly warning or hostile. The vague disquietude that prevailed had so much affected Lillian that she kept thinking about the past adventure, what could have been done differently, and if they had forgotten or missed something important while dealing with Dina.

Jack and Sawyer noticed her absent-mindedness, but they let Lillian be. Why bother her now? She was the only one who knew enough of the archeology and the ancient Egyptian language to know what was important or meaningful at the camp. Jack knew only a few words of the old language and hieroglyphs, and Sawyer knew none. They had all been pulled into the previous adventure because of Dina and Lillian's interest in archeology. She had exchanged letters with Sir Michael Merriweather before she came to Egypt.

Sir Michael had set up the camp with his younger colleague Lewis Llewellyn near the German camp led by Walther Wolfe with his assistant Carl Manheim. All of them were dead now, killed by Dina, the demon or evil spirit, awakened when they opened the tomb.

Staring at the distance and the vast dunescape, Lillian thought about the tomb's curse. She didn't know what the two archeologist groups, the Brits and the Germans, had found inside. She suspected they had read hieroglyphs, and that had released Dina. However, now that Lillian had reconsidered the past events, perhaps simply opening the tomb had been enough to wake Dina, the demon. She hoped to find clues about what the Germans had found outside the tomb, like drawings, hieroglyphs, images, or anything else. The German archeologists would have recorded all the details of the exterior walls of the tomb and if they had discovered anything else during the excavation outside.

Sawyer put his hand on Jack's arm and said, "Slow down. We have to approach the camps carefully. Let me go there first and check out the area. I don't want to drive into the arms of the Schutzstaffel or Afrikakorps."

Jack parked further away, and they studied the area. Everything looked abandoned. The closest camp was the German one. Its tents were ripped in the stormy wind, and the sand had piled against the openings of the tents. No footprints were visible, but then the wind blew the sand and covered any prints in minutes.

Paling, Jack recalled how Dina had decided that he was of no use to her and tried to sink him into a quicksand pit. He would have been dead within seconds if it had been her sister who had pledged to Dina and made her stop.

Sawyer took off and walked towards the tents. When he got closer, he glanced inside each tent, seeing nothing but sand, left behind items like books, tables, chairs, and maps. All looked undisturbed, as if they had been there for a while. He went back outside and waved his hand to Jack, who drove closer and picked him up.

They couldn't see the British archeologists' camp from there, so Jack drove on, recalling well the last time he had arrived at that camp and met Dina in the body of Lewis

Llewellyn. It had been a weird and horrifying encounter that he didn't want to experience again.

The British camp looked exactly like it had when Lillian and Jack were there the last time. This time Lillian jumped off the Jeep and walked towards the main tent where she had seen the books and maps the last time. The sand sunk under each step, and it was heavy to walk.

While approaching the three tents, Sir Michael's tent, the cook's tent, and the third one that had belonged to Llewellyn, she didn't see any prints or signs that anyone had been there since her last visit.

The Brits had arrived after the Germans. They had not brought any local workers, so their tents were not close by. The Germans had found the tomb and started the excavation, and thus, their local workers had stayed closer to the archeological site and not where the archeologists stayed.

Lillian pushed away the fabric flap of the tent's opening and entered the dim interior. She looked around and saw books, papyruses, and maps scattered on the floor after the storm. She thought some papyruses must have gotten lost in the storm wind and crouched to gather the documents and pile them on the table.

The British Camp

"**I**'ll wait here and keep an eye on everything," Sawyer said, pushing his hat backward.

Jack followed Lillian inside. He glanced around. *Empty and in disarray*, he thought. *Good, perhaps no one was here after we left.*

Lillian looked at her brother and then continued gathering and piling the documents and books on the table. "I'll gather all here, then sift through," she explained.

Jack nodded and said, "I can help. You start reading and going through that pile, and I'll look around what else I can find." He crouched down, moved the dirt and sand around, and found some more items buried under the piled-up sand, including some leatherbound books and a pipe.

Lillian pulled a chair closer to the table and sat down. She took the first book and read the first page to learn its title, as the covers were too worn and scratched to read. It was a history of ancient Egypt. *Could be useful*, she thought and put it aside. The next one was a book explaining hieroglyphs written by Sir Michael himself. *Definitely useful*. She put it on the pile to take with her.

"Take a look at this," Jack said, handing her a leather-bound notebook. "This might be what you were looking for. The last page is dated the day when they went to open the tomb."

Lillian grabbed it and quickly opened it. It was written by Llewellyn, Sir Michael's assistant. He must have kept a diary because the notebook started when they had arrived in Cairo two days before they had bought the camels and rode here.

Lillian kept reading. Llewellyn wrote that they had met the German archeologists, and Sir Michael had made a deal with them. They would jointly open the tomb and share the discovery of the new tomb and the treasures inside because the Germans had not enough local workers, whereas Sir Michael could acquire plenty more with his contacts. Llewellyn mentioned that this archeological site had been difficult to excavate because the locals worked there only for a day and then disappeared at night. The progress had been slower than Walther had expected, he had written. The last note was that they were going to the tomb after breakfast and nothing after that.

"No, this wasn't helpful. If we had found the notes from the Germans, then that would have been valuable," Lillian said and put the notebook away.

Perhaps Llewellyn's family would like to have it as a keepsake. I could ship it to them or give it to Ambassador Hare to send back to England to Llewellyn's family, she considered. She frowned and picked up the next volume from the pile. Another book on the history of Egypt. *If I have room, I can take this one too*, she thought.

She checked each book carefully. Some were autographed by Sir Michael, and some belonged to Llewellyn. While they were interesting to read, they were not unique and didn't solve the puzzle of the bat or the uneasiness she had felt yesterday. Something was off, and she knew it.

Jack was on his hands and knees, searching the items and papers on the floor. When he had passed the tent's area twice and found nothing else, he stood up, brushed his pants clean from the sand, stepped to the table, pulled another chair, and sat next to Lillian. "How is it going? Did you find anything?"

"No, not yet. I see you found some maps and papyruses. Perhaps they contain something interesting. Let's take them with us. I'm done here. I'll take these books with me, and those others can stay here. There wasn't anything of value in them." Lillian grabbed three books and the notebook in her arms, and Jack took the stack of papyruses and maps with him. The bright sunshine and the hot wind hit them when they stepped outside.

Sawyer sat in the jeep. When he heard their voices approaching, his eyes turned to Lillian and Jack. He climbed off the vehicle, quickly walked to Lillian to help her with the books, and took them to the jeep's trunk.

"Let's go to the German camp," Lillian said. "They found the tomb first, so they might have something useful in their tents."

"Yes, you're right. They found it, so how did they discover it?" Jack said, agreeing. "Did they read it in some document or accidentally stumble upon it."

"Yes, those are the questions that interest me too," Sawyer said while Jack started the car and drove towards the other camp.

"If Dina orchestrated the whole discovery and the opening of her tomb, then we should find some clues in the German camp," Jack added.

Chapter 12

The Bat

The wind had picked up, and the sand swirled around them when Jack drove towards the German camp. When they had the camp in their sight, a shadow passed them.

Jack glanced up and swerved when he saw a bird-like figure flying above them, heading in the same direction as they were. But it wasn't a bird. *It's the ugly bat again,* he thought.

"The bat!" Sawyer said. He ducked down because the bat flew low over them and would have hit with his wings at his head. "That evil creature is after me," Sawyer complained and crouched lower inside the car, watching the next circling of the bat.

Veering and turning, the bat made a second attempt to attack Sawyer, who leaned right and then tried to hit it with his binoculars with no luck.

The bat glared at Sawyer with its human-like eyes, his blackish wings flapped in the wind, and it floated next to the vehicle while keeping its eyes on Sawyer. Shrieking, it opened his mouth, and Sawyer could see the saliva dripping from the sharp teeth. "That bat is too human to be real," he muttered.

"I agree," Lillian said and stared at the bat.

"Bats should not be out during the daylight, but he is," Sawyer replied, trying to swat the bat again with his binoculars.

Jack veered to the left when the bat flew directly above him. "Keep it away. I'm trying to steer this car, and that bat has plans to get rid of us. If he keeps doing those overpasses, I might lose control of this car, and it might tumble over in the dunes," Jack warned.

"The camp is over there. If we get there before the next attack, we can all enter the tent. Maybe it will stay outside," Lillian shouted.

Jack pressed the gas pedal, and the car lurched over the next dune, and for a short moment, the bat stayed behind, surprised by the sudden speed increase. It didn't fool the bat for long because it continued its chase.

Jack parked in front of the main tent, which had belonged to the renowned German archeologist Walther Wolfe. They climbed out of the car and rushed inside the tent.

Jack closed the tent's opening after them with the strings and pulled a table in front of the opening too. He didn't believe it would help much, but hopefully, it would slow the flying beast.

They saw the huge shadow approaching the tent, fly by, and circle it. Then it flew and hit the fabric, which didn't tear but bounced, then ricocheted back.

"Watch out! The bat is doing a second attack!" Sawyer called as he saw the bat going around again and trying to enter through the blocked opening. The bat cried angrily as it hit the fabric, and its claws pierced it, leaving two slits behind.

"We have to get that bat. It will attack again," Jack said, looking inside the tent for a tool to use against the bat. "We can't use our pistols. I don't know how far the sound of a shot would echo in this wind, and I don't want the Germans to find out we are here."

He took the heavy wooden chair. "How about using the legs of this chair and hitting the bat?" Sawyer and Jack stepped on the chair, broke the legs off, took each leg, and handed one to Lillian.

Through the tent's fabric, they saw a large shadow flying towards them and heard the angry, menacing shriek.

Positioning next to the tent's wall, they all raised their chair legs and waited for the right moment. When the bat flew against the fabric again, Sawyer and Jack hit its body and wings.

The bat struggled and fell to the ground near the tent's opening. Sawyer and Jack saw how it crawled away, dragging one bent wing behind it. "We got it. It won't bother us for a while," Sawyer assured Lillian, who sighed and smiled.

"Good, now I can get back to work."

Chapter 13

In the Tent

"What is that bat?" Jack asked. "It isn't a normal bat. It must have followed us, and now it's attacking like it doesn't want us to be here."

Sawyer nodded. "I think it's some kind of evil spirit that has taken the form of an ugly bat, like how Dina took the body of the archeologist first and then the young woman's in the blimp."

Lillian glanced at the men and added, "I believe you are correct. Also, that bat knows there's something here in this tent that it wants or does not want us to discover. And I want to find out what it is."

She looked at the books and collected piles of papers and papyri on the table. Jack went to help her while Sawyer stood by the tent's opening and kept an eye on the outside in case the bat or anyone else approached.

Jack looked around at the ground again. He dug in the sand piled up around the tent and found a small bone buried there, which he picked up and took to the table. "This was on the ground."

Lillian looked at it closely. "A bone. It could belong to a human, a finger bone perhaps."

"Show me," Sawyer asked, and Jack took the bone to him.

"Yes, it's a finger bone." He glanced at Lillian and asked, "Could this be what the bat was after? You said it didn't want us to find something."

Lillian frowned. "It's possible. This bone might belong to its body if it is a spirit from the underworld. Perhaps it can't muster enough power to be like Dina unless all the bones are in one place or one sarcophagus." She viewed the papers again and found Carl Manheim's notes of the tomb they had found. "This is it," she muttered and quickly read the handwritten notes in German. "He's describing how they found the tomb. They had found a papyrus that described a hidden tomb near the Valley of the Kings, but not in the valley. They had searched other areas, then came here, and after one sandstorm, the tomb had revealed itself."

Jack looked at Lillian. "So, it's possible that Dina or Anubis led the German archeologist to this place."

"Yes, it is." Lillian continued reading. "They had sent daily reports to Berlin to Himmler's headquarters. On the first day, they saw a peak of a tomb uncovered from the sand. When they dug around it, they found a small bone and some more human bones around it. They thought they had found another burial site. However, upon closer study of the bones, they realized they were all hundreds of years old. And what was even stranger, the bones seemed to belong to one person. They marked here that the bones were scattered like the animals or something else had parted the body parts and bones in different directions. They had gathered bones in the excavation area in front of the tomb's opening when the British archeologists arrived. They had not told them about the bones they had found. Walther had instructed Carl to keep it a secret. The Brits thought that the large excavation area in front of the tomb was just to reveal the tomb's sides and find the doorway to the tomb."

Lillian glanced up. "So, this happened the day before we arrived based on the date of the notes. The next morning all the archeologists and their crew were killed. We arrived at the British camp after that."

Jack nodded. "The timeline sounds good." He gestured at the bone and asked, "If that's one of the bones they found, then where are the rest?"

"I believe they are in the excavation area. This is the only one here that is not there," Lillian replied and took the bone in her hand. "Perhaps, this is why the bat followed us and then wanted to enter the tent. He sensed we had found what he was looking for."

"It's all guessing until we know for sure," Sawyer said impatiently. "Grab all the stuff you have found, and let's go. I don't want to be here longer than necessary. We need to find a place to overnight or go back to Cairo to our hotel."

Lillian nodded and gathered the maps, hieroglyphs, and books in her arms, and Jack took some other volumes from the table with them, and they left the tent.

The bat was nowhere to be seen. It was like it had never existed.

The sun shone high up in the sky, and the heat was rising. They packed all the books in the car and then climbed inside, and Jack drove away from the camp. "Cairo or somewhere else?" Jack asked, turning his head to Lillian and Sawyer.

"It does not feel safe here with the Germans digging by the tomb and the bat attacking us, so I would vote going back to Cairo," Lillian replied.

Sawyer nodded. "Yes, we don't know what we are facing yet. Lillian should read the documents and notes first and see if there are more clues about what could be going on. I vote Cairo too."

"Okay, that's where we'll go then," Jack replied.

Chapter 14

The Past Crimes

1300 BC in Ancient Egypt

The palace was in chaos after Pharaoh Akhenaten returned sooner than expected from his trip to the river Nile.

His high priest, Thutmose, knew something was wrong because his daughter Dina had locked herself inside her room. She was pledged to be a virgin and soon to be offered to Hapi, the god of the river Nile, for a bountiful year and the god Min, for plentiful crops for the coming season. Pharaoh Akhenaten would take her away to the sacrificial site upon his arrival.

Thutmose was a lean man with a bald head. He bore the symbols of priesthood in his white robe and wore a jewel-decorated broad-collar necklace and golden bracelets decorated with images of the Egyptian gods. As a high priest, he was responsible for reading the Black Book of Anubis and the Golden Book of Ra and interpreting the gods' wishes and prophecies. The lower priests were chosen to help with menial tasks like writing hieroglyphs, readying the sacrificial animals and humans, and preparing the dead for their travel to the underworld.

Frowning, he asked the three pharaoh's guards in the hallway to help him open the heavy door. They put aside their spears and pushed the door with their shoulders over and over again until it broke open. They stumbled inside, quickly turning their faces to the ground. Thutmose waved at them to leave the room.

When Thutmose entered, his heart skipped a beat as his daughter, Dina, had destroyed her life and future. She had betrayed the pharaoh and the gods. She had slept with the slave, Aper.

Dina turned her dark eyes to her father rebelliously. Her bead-decorated and braided black hair reached past her shoulders to her hips. Her eyes were shadowed with black kohl, and her lips were colored with red ochre. Her blue dress, decorated with golden threads made especially for the sacrifice ceremony, lay on the floor by the bedside.

The slave, Aper, rose from the bed and bowed his head. Thutmose was a powerful man in the palace, and Aper knew he had committed a crime and waited for the punishment. He knew he couldn't run or escape. The pharaoh was at the gates of his palace, and he was too powerful to escape from. His soldiers would find him fast if Aper would even try to run. And the pharaoh's revenge would be dreadful, worse than what it would be now.

Thutmose went outside and left the lovers guarded. The pharaoh's entourage had just arrived, and Thutmose had the unpleasant task of telling the pharaoh the bad news.

"My pharaoh, my daughter Dina is no longer suitable for the sacrifice," Thutmose said, keeping his eyes on the floor. He was not allowed to look into the pharaoh's eyes. The pharaoh was a god on earth.

Akhenaten told Thutmose that his daughter Dina would be buried alive in the new tomb they had built. There was only one sentence for a slave: death.

When the day arrived for the slave to die, Thutmose took his morning ritual bath to clean himself, then with the help of slaves, he got dressed in his most impressive high priest's outfit: A white robe with golden adornments of the ancient symbols. He took his high priest symbols: the scepter decorated with golden wings, and the black book of Anubis, the god of the dead, with him. This was the day for the curses and to pray for Anubis to help his daughter Dina. Thutmose blamed the slave. He was certain that it was the slave who had seduced his daughter and, thus, did not deserve to live, whereas his daughter would have been innocent of the crime and should not have been punished so harshly.

Her slave lover had been whipped earlier that morning with a leather whip. Now, he was waiting for his death.

A large crowd had gathered along the river Nile to see the rare execution. It was not every day that a high priest's daughter would be killed by her father. The pharaoh would also come to see the execution of the slave and the entombment of Dina, who had betrayed the pharaoh and the gods.

The pharaoh's soldiers escorted Aper to the place of his sentencing, where he waited in a plain white loincloth, his hands tied in front of him. The guards stood next to him in full body armor with spears in their hands. When Thutmose came to the riverside, the guards pushed Aper to his knees, and he kept his eyes on the ground. His strong upper body shone with sweat. Red welts and dried blood streaked his back from a recent whipping.

The heat was rising as the sun scorched the dry land.

The crowd silenced and fell to the ground when the pharaoh's entourage arrived. He had only two hundred slaves accompanying him and sat on a golden throne carried by his favorite slaves. He wore the golden robe of the king, emblazoned with black images of the gods of Egypt, and had his blue Khepresh crown on. The king's insignia was a rearing cobra called the Uraeus, attached to the very front of the pharaoh's crown. It symbolized the protective goddess Wadjet.

Thutmose kneeled and bowed his head as Pharaoh Akhenaten approached the riverside. Dina also kneeled, bowed, and raised her hands to Akhenaten and pleaded for mercy, which the pharaoh denied.

Aper turned his eyes to Dina and called to her, "Dina, my love, my god's gift. I will meet you in the afterlife."

But the pharaoh did not want to hear this, and thus Akhenaten's eyes turned angry, and he said, "No, you won't. Your head will be separated, and your limbs will be torn off your body. Your body parts will be scattered in the desert. No soul will find its way when it is torn apart."

Dina's face distorted in agony, and she shivered in fear. She had hoped to meet Aper in the other life, but the pharaoh squashed that hope. Her fear turned into anger towards the people of Egypt and the pharaoh who sentenced the lovers. She silently swore that she would get revenge for her lover and their lives as she cried out to Aper, "I love you. I will find you. I will bring your soul back to live with me."

Thutmose turned to the guards and nodded. At the same moment, the guards lifted their swords and cut off the slave's head, and then proceeded to hack off his limbs from his body. The crowd murmured quietly as they watched the riverbank turn red from the blood of the slave.

The guards tied a rope to each limb, climbed on their horses, and Pharaoh Akhenaten lifted his flail and lowered it, giving the sign to go. The guards rode toward the desert, pulling the body parts on a rope behind their horses. The dust cloud formed behind them, and soon, they were out of sight. Each body part was left in a different location where the animals would gnaw and eat them, and the bones would disappear into the sand and be forgotten.

Next, Thutmose went to the tomb with his daughter and told her he would ask Anubis to help her get her revenge. He read the Black Book of Anubis and asked him to help Dina. He left the tomb, hoping that the god had listened to him. Dina's tomb was closed while she was left alive inside. Anubis heard Thutmose, but he also heard the previous plea made by Dina and Aper. The lovers wanted to meet in the afterlife, but the pharaoh denied their request. Anubis was the ruler of the underworld, and thus he decided that if Dina was going to get her revenge, Aper should have a chance too. If even one of his bones was returned to Dina's tomb, he could return to life like Dina. That was Anubis's decision.

It was unlikely that any of the scattered body parts would be found or brought to the cursed tomb. Still, if someday that happened, Aper would have his revenge and join his lover Dina in the underworld when his retaliation against Egypt and its rulers was completed.

Chapter 15

The Duat

The Duat and the spirit's journey in the afterlife in Ancient Egypt

Normally, the deceased who died in ancient Egypt were mummified, or if you died inside a tomb, the deceased spirit would travel to Duat and then forward to meet Osiris, the dead king of the netherworld.

Aper was never mummified or died inside a tomb. Thus, he was denied the pathway to the afterlife. His body was torn apart, and his body parts were scattered in the desert.

In the underworld, Anubis stood by the gates protecting the entrance. The god had the scales of justice on his one hand, and he waited for the recently dead to arrive to weigh their hearts to see if they were worthy to enter the afterlife. The heart, which contained all the deeds of the deceased, was weighed against the feather of the goddess Ma'at, the symbol of virtue, truth, and justice.

If the heart didn't pass this test and was heavier than the feather, it was fed to Ammut, the Devourer. Ammut was a demon with the forequarters of a lion, the hindquarters of a hippopotamus, and the head of a crocodile. And after that, the failed spirit was thrown into the darkness. If the spirit passed the test, it could meet Osiris. The king of the afterworld welcomed the spirits into the afterlife. It reflected life in the real world with a similar landscape, gods, and tasks to do in the Fields of Rushes, the idealized view of life on Earth.

Dina was not mummified, but she died inside the tomb, so her path to the underworld was secured, and Anubis granted her father's wish for her revenge. Thutmose had read the right incantations from the Black Book of Anubis to earn Dina this chance.

A deadly love affair between the priest's daughter and a slave was so rare that even the gods heard about it. And because Anubis was the one who tested the hearts of the deceased, he decided that Aper's crime was not heavy to condemn him to eternal darkness.

Dina loved Aper when they were both alive. It had not been just a whim of a rich daughter of the high priest but genuine love. Aper returned the feeling and was ready to give his life if they were caught, and they were.

Now, as Dina was in limbo, not cast in the darkness with lost souls and not moving forward to eternal life, she had time to find out what happened to Aper. She spied Anubis and discovered that Aper had a chance if one of his bones would be found and taken to the tomb. Then his spirit could travel to the afterlife.

Deciding to help Aper, Dina figured out a way to intercept the events in the living world. She had learned a lot of the rules of the underworld while waiting for her time of revenge.

The boundaries between the living and the dead were thinnest after sunset, so Dina chose a bat who preferred flying at nighttime. Dina captured this large creature of the night and poured her spirit into it. She was allowed to do that because she was not doomed or saved in the afterlife.

In her search for Aper's remains, Dina found out that her old helpers, Lillian, Jack, and Sawyer, were back in Cairo, so she went to haunt them. Revengefully, Dina chased them and blocked all Roy Sawyer's romantic moments. He was supposed to be her slave in the world where she ruled! Instead, this man was smooching other women.

She knew that Lillian was an archeologist, so she followed Lillian to the camp, recognizing the bone of Aper. Dina tried to grab it but failed. The humans had blocked the entrance of the tent, so she could not enter, then they hit the bat, thus making flying impossible with a broken wing. Dina left the bat and returned to the underworld to follow the events from there. She hoped Lillian would take the bone to the tomb with her and save Aper. Otherwise, Dina would have to catch another bat and find another of Aper's bones. It would be a difficult, almost impossible task because Aper had died centuries ago. Dina would recognize the bones because she didn't see them as the humans did, just bare bones, but recognized whom they had belonged to.

Chapter 16

The Germans

1940, Egypt

Jack drove the car t the same way they had before, but that was not a good idea. They only reached halfway when two Jeeps and a tank swirled ahead of them behind the dunes. The two vehicles had black-clad officers and two soldiers with Afrikakorps brown uniforms in each car.

Jack slowed and turned his Jeep to veer around them.

"Halt!" one of the soldiers shouted.

Of course, Jack knew what it meant. There was no reason to pretend that he didn't. If any soldiers and officers knew them, they would know they were pretending not to understand. Besides, Jack and Sawyer had sat in Hotel Alhambra's bar for months since they returned from the Alps, so any of these soldiers could have seen them there and knew they spoke German.

Their Panzer tank looked ominous as it moved its gun and aimed it at Jack, Lillian, and Sawyer.

Jack slowed down and stopped. No need to risk their lives. Jack raised his hands, showing that he'd given up, and so did the others.

The German officer climbed out of their vehicle, brushing the invisible dust and sand off his knee-length pants. His boots were black and so shiny you could see your image on them. He had a crossbelt over his impeccable black uniform and a pistol holster on the belt. His SS-staff officer visor cap was made from dark wool with a leather sweatband and an eagle, and a skull and cross bones (Totenkopf) symbol attached in the front of it.

Sawyer whispered, "Don't do anything rash. Don't give any information freely. Let's find out first what they know and what they want."

Jack nodded almost imperceptibly.

The officer took his time. He had a high forehead and narrow face with metal-rimmed glasses.

He gestured to the soldier to follow him. The soldier got up, holding his rifle ready, and they both walked toward Jack.

"Guten tag," the officer greeted them. "My name is Gruppenführer Karl Altmann." He gestured for them to lower their hands, and they did so.

Jack nodded but didn't say a word, nor did Lillian or Sawyer.

Altmann's sharp blue eyes moved from Jack to Lillian and finally to Sawyer. "I assume you are the three Brits that had an...adventure in Berlin and also at the Alps," he commented casually.

Sawyer rolled his eyes. An adventure with a demon! What a choice of words.

"SS-Reichsführer Himmler informed me that I might meet you here," the officer added, tilting his head and viewing each one in the vehicle again. "He said that you met the supernatural power and possessed it. Our leader is very interested in getting his hands on such a power as you might know."

Jack tapped the wheel with his fingers, keeping his eyes downcast. Lillian leaned on the window and didn't look at the officer. Sawyer was the only one who met Altmann's eyes. They stared at each other for a long time without a word.

The silent exchange was both interesting and threatening.

Sawyer was not sure if he was staring at a cobra readying to strike or a harmless garden snake. He suspected it was the former rather than the latter because SS officers did not have the reputation of being nice or kind.

Finally, Altmann said, "I would like you to come with me to the excavation area near the tomb where the supernatural being came from. I think you might be of use to us."

He didn't give them a chance to say no. Instead, he walked back to his car. And they left, heading to the excavation area.

Chapter 17

Prisoners Again

1940, Egypt

Gruppenführer Karl Altmann, a commanding presence in the Nazi hierarchy, disembarked from his vehicle with swift precision as soon as it came to a halt. His gaze latched onto Jack's jeep, an intensity that didn't escape Jack's notice as he sighed and parked adjacent to his own vehicle.

With a nonchalant gesture of his right hand, Altmann snapped his fingers, summoning a cadre of soldiers who promptly encircled the jeep and its occupants. Lillian, undeterred, gracefully brushed loose strands of hair from her face. Her eyes traversed the scene, moving from the stern faces of the German soldiers to their leader, and then beyond him to the excavation site that housed Dina's ancient tomb. It was a proximity she had never experienced before, and the sight of the Germans meticulously uncovering the tomb's sides left an indelible impression.

The once-concealed tomb now lay exposed, as well as the area around it. The meticulous efforts of the German soldiers and their workers had revealed all facets of the tomb, and the exposed area bore witness to the bone-chilling evidence of past lives—piles of skeletal remains, remnants of the deceased, neatly arranged to one side of the excavation.

As Lillian's eyes darted around the area, she realized how much the Germans had already discovered. They could soon unearth not just bones but the very essence of the supernatural mysteries that lay dormant within the tomb's ancient walls. A compelling desire stirred within Lillian as she stood in the proximity of the ancient tomb. The hieroglyphs, etched onto the weathered surface, beckoned to her like cryptic whispers from the past. A longing to decipher the enigmatic symbols seized her, prompting a fervent wish to approach and closely examine the intricacies of the tomb's inscriptions.

The prospect of reading the inscriptions held a magnetic allure for Lillian. She pondered whether she might recognize any familiar phrases or symbols, particularly harboring the hope of deciphering a potential curse. The notion lingered in her mind—what if the curse lay hidden within, an arcane script that, when unleashed, could free Dina from the confines of the underworld? The mere act of opening the tomb, undertaken by unwitting archaeologists, could unwittingly trigger a curse, setting in motion a series of events that might liberate the ancient spirit haunting the shadows of history.

Her thoughts danced on the precipice of the extraordinary and the inexplicable, weaving a tapestry of speculation and fascination. As she contemplated the hieroglyphs adorning the tomb, Lillian grappled with the anticipation of unraveling a tale both haunting and powerful, a narrative etched into the stone by the hands of those long gone. The tomb stood as a silent sentinel, guarding secrets that begged to be unveiled, and Lillian found herself standing at the threshold, torn between caution and the relentless pursuit of knowledge.

Jack folded his arms in front of him and stared at the leader of the Germans angrily. "What do you want from us?"

Karl Altman turned his head slightly and glanced at him as if he was just an irritating bug buzzing around him.

Lillian glanced towards the tan-colored tents that the Germans had near the excavation area. She saw a sturdy man with a huge mustache and a big potbelly emerging from the tent. He wore shiny black boots, black knee-length pants, and a black shirt with a crossbelt. He wiped his forehead with a large white handkerchief before advancing in their direction.

Sawyer and Jack glanced at each other. It was obvious that man was the reason they were here, but who was he, and what did the Germans want from them? They were civilians, and although they were their enemies, Egypt had not been a hostile area for different nationalities unless the Germans decided otherwise. Then both men's gazes flickered to Lillian, who was still admiring the tomb and not paying attention to the man approaching them.

"Lillian!" Jack called her name, and she quickly turned her head to her brother. He nodded towards the man, and Lillian turned her gaze to him.

"I know him," Lillian uttered softly. Both Jack and Sawyer shifted their gaze to the man capturing Lillian's attention before turning their eyes back to her. "Who is he?" Jack inquired.

"The gentleman there is Helmut Hoffmeister, the director of the German National Museum. He conducted research on Egyptian artifacts before the war," Lillian elaborated, her gaze fixed on Helmut. "I had the opportunity to meet him in London before the war," she added.

"That could be the reason for his presence. He likely learned of your being here in Egypt, and expressed a desire to meet you," Jack proposed, pointing out the apparent connection.

Sawyer nodded. "The Germans have spies, and our recent escapade in Berlin has not gone without notice."

Lillian considered the possibility, acknowledging, "It's certainly within the realm of possibility."

In response to the unspoken invitation, Helmut confidently approached their small group. With a genial smile adorning his face, he extended his somewhat pudgy and perspiring hand toward Lillian. "How utterly charming to meet you again, Ms. Stiller," he greeted, his voice resonating with a mix of familiarity and courtesy.

Lillian took his hand, and he quickly kissed on top of her hand like a gentleman. Lillian smiled widely. "Mr. Hoffmeister, let me introduce you to my brother Jack, and this is Roy Sawyer."

Helmut barely took his eyes off Lillian when he said, "Please call me Helmut. I'm a colonel in the Gestapo nowadays. War changes everything." When his eyes finally turned to Lillian's company, his eyes were fishlike cold staring at them without any friendliness. His words did not match his eyes when he said, "Nice to meet you too. Let us go to my tent where it's cooler. I have some things to discuss with Ms. Stiller."

Lillian quickly replied, "Lillian, please."

Helmut extended his arm to Lillian, who took it smiling, and they walked towards the tent area. Jack and Sawyer were about to follow when the soldiers ran in front of them and barricaded the way. Jack took a step backward and said to Sawyer, "It looks like the invitation was only to Lillian."

Sawyer scratched his chin and glanced at Karl Altman, who stood guarding the vehicles. "Can we go to the tent too?"

Altman turned and replied, "The invitation was not to you but to her. She's the archeologist. You are the extra workforce." Then he gestured to the excavation area where the locals were carrying bones and piling them to the side of the camp and added, "That's your job."

All the bones were from the workers and archeologists who had died at Dina's hand when she was released. The black beetles had devoured all the flesh from the bodies leaving skeletons behind. That's why the workers were now moving away so that the archeological location could be properly examined.

Chapter 18

What Helmut Wants

Lillian turned her head, glanced back, and saw the soldiers stopping his brother and Sawyer. She turned to Helmut and asked, "What's going on? Why don't you let my brother and Sawyer join us?"

"They aren't archeologists, so I don't need them. I need your knowledge." Helmut put his arm over her shoulders and led her toward his large tent. "Inside, please. I will explain everything to you." He pushed Lillian inside in front of him.

"Ah, better. This heat will be the death of me," Helmut muttered and walked directly to the small table with glasses and bottles. He took a bottle of water, poured it into his glass, and then drank it. He didn't offer anything to Lillian, who stood still, hands shoved in her pockets, and stared at Helmut under furrowed brows.

"What do you want from me?"

Helmut's eyes flickered to her, and without immediate reply, he walked to a chair and sat down. He stared at Lillian for a long time, and his unfriendly stare made Lillian feel chilly even though it was hot, like in the sauna. "What I want is for you to help me to bring back the supernatural being, the demon who accompanied you to Berlin. If you do that, you, your brother, and the other man will be freed."

Lillian gaped at him. "Why would I do that?" She shook her head. "I don't even know if it is possible to get her back. She didn't finish her task on Earth and is now in the underworld. I have no idea how she could re-enter this world."

Helmut's voice was steely when he replied, "You better figure it out because that's the only reason you'll be alive with your companions. We don't need you if you don't assist us. Our leader is extremely interested in all paranormal and supernatural powers, and Dina was exactly what he was looking for."

Lillian swallowed hard. She had to think of something and fast. She couldn't let Dina return, but she didn't want to let Helmut know that. It would be a death sentence for all of them. She went along with Helmut's plan and said, "I don't have any clue how to assist Dina's return. I must see her tomb inside and outside to see how she was originally entombed and released."

Lillian recalled the bone they had found in the camp. She still had it in her pocket, where she had stuffed it when the Germans blocked their way back to Cairo. She fingered it. She couldn't be hundred percent sure, but this bone in her pocket could be hundreds of years old. She recalled the report she had read in the old German camp that they had found bones belonging to one person but scattered around the desert in front of the tomb. Could these bones and Dina's death have something in common?

One thing was sure: The tomb was the only place where she would get more answers to her questions and to this man who kept her now as his prisoner.

She sighed. "I'd like to have a drink. It's a hot day. I will perform better if I'm not dehydrated."

"Of course, Lillian," Helmut said, standing up and walking to the table to pour her a glass of water. He turned and handed the glass to her. She sipped it slowly.

Helmut said, "I'm glad that you are sensible. We'll work well together."

Chapter 19

Lillian and Helmut

L illian sat down, considering her choices. She was imprisoned in the camp of the leader of the Axis powers, and she was an enemy to them. Also, Helmut's threat that she would be killed if she didn't help concerned her. Usually, the army would take prisoners and not kill them, but Helmut was part of the Gestapo. Their infamous reputation was whispered about in the cities the Germans had conquered. They were known to torture the Allied soldiers, suspected spies, and the known supporters of Jews.

Lillian wondered if they would really kill her if she refused to work for them. She didn't want to test that. Helmut might resort to cruelty if she started arguing, and she didn't want that. He might torture her brother and Sawyer instead of her to make her comply with his demands.

Wondering what she should do next, Lillian kept her eyes on her glass and brushed a lock of her brown hair back behind her ear. She didn't want anything to happen to her or her companions. She knew her brother and Roy Sawyer were taken away but didn't know where or for what. She turned her head and asked Helmut, "What happened to my brother and Sawyer?" She tried to keep her face emotionless because she didn't want Helmut to see how much she cared for both men.

Helmut hadn't taken his eyes off her after sitting in a wooden chair on the other side of the table. Now he leaned forward and replied, "They will be camp workers with the other local workers. This is a work camp, not a leisure camp. They will have to do their part, or they will be punished. He paused and added. "And don't think I won't retort to violence if your work does not, please me." His eyes looked mean when he added the last part. "I have my party leaders to answer to, and I don't want to disappoint them."

Frowning, Lillian looked at him. "I can't help if the tomb does not reveal its secrets. Perhaps there is no way to recall the demon back to life." She crossed her fingers, hoping what she said was true as she didn't want to meet Dina ever again.

Helmut stared at her, his eyes cold like dead fish. "You better hope you can find something because I'm not going back to Berlin with no results."

He didn't add that it would be a disgrace and a demotion if his superiors were kind. He knew the party leaders could be rash in their judgment, and they could send him to Russia's war front, and that was almost the same as a death sentence. He stood up and said, "You have rested enough inside my tent. It's time for you to go to work. My soldiers will keep an eye on you, and I want daily reports." With these words, he took a few steps to the tent's opening and gestured for two soldiers to come.

When the soldiers stopped and greeted him with their right hand raised in front of them, lowered their hands, and stood still waiting for orders, Helmut nodded. He raised his right hand, lowered it, and explained what he wanted. "This woman is now a valuable prisoner. Keep an eye on her. You will pay with your lives if she escapes, dies, or gets hurt." He gestured toward the tomb and said, "Take her to the tomb. She can start with the external hieroglyphs and images and see if that brings us any closer to the supernatural mystery of this tomb."

The soldiers clicked their heels and greeted again with a raised hand, and then grabbed Lillian by the arms and walked her away. Lillian tried to struggle free from their hold, but it was of no use. She dragged her feet and tried to go slowly in the sand. The soldiers pulled her mercilessly forward. When she passed the excavation camp, she saw her brother Jack and Roy Sawyer digging sand and separating everything from what they discovered into boxes: bones and artifacts. They had to check the skeletons' mouths for gold teeth and take them to a separate box reserved for the valuable items.

As Lillian moved through the bustling activity of the workers, a disconcerting realization dawned upon her. The skeletal remains scattered across the excavation site weren't solely comprised of local individuals who had met their demise; among them lay the silent witnesses to a darker chapter in history—archaeologists who had perished when the tomb was first unveiled. Discerning the distinct attire adorning the deceased, she noted the juxtaposition of local tunics with more modern clothing worn by the German and English skeletons.

The macabre scene further unfolded as she encountered newly added bodies, their flesh, skin, hair, and garments still intact. A morbid suspicion gripped Lillian; these were recent casualties, victims of a sinister turn of events. The presence of freshly deceased individuals suggested that the Germans, in their relentless pursuit of archaeological treasures, had resorted to eliminating potential threats—be they perceived enemies, grave robbers, or workers who proved unwilling or untrustworthy. The excavation site bore witness to a chilling tableau of lives sacrificed in the pursuit of forbidden knowledge, underscoring the ominous toll exacted by the quest for the supernatural secrets concealed within the ancient tomb.

Chapter 20

The Exterior of the Tomb

L illian nodded to Jack and Sawyer as she was escorted past them. She couldn't say anything because she believed the German soldiers would stop her, but she tried to look reassuring.

It was a hot day, and the sand was burning hot.

Both Sawyer and Jack looked exhausted after an hour of work. Their backs and armpits were soaking wet. They were not used to working in this kind of weather like the locals. She recalled that Sawyer had been in the Foreign League, so he might be better adjusted to the desert weather than Jack. However, since Sawyer had left the league, he'd been a smuggler and a frequent visitor in various Cairo bars, so Lillian didn't believe he was ready for the hard labor the German requested. Jack wasn't. That was certain. He was used to London's mild climate with frequent fog and rain.

Lillian worried that Jack and Sawyer would be dehydrated or pass out soon if the Germans didn't give them enough water to drink or a break in a shady area. He glimpsed at the soldiers escorting her and asked, "Are you going to give the workers any breaks or water to drink? It's a hot day."

The soldiers looked stern. The other one said, "Weiter gehen," and pushed her back with his other hand. Lillian stumbled. *So, this is how it is. I will be pushed around and told to go on, and I won't get any answers,* she fumed. Lillian knew she couldn't do anything because the soldiers were armed, and she wasn't.

The soldiers stopped twenty feet from the tomb's exterior wall and gestured for Lillian to proceed. Giving them an angry scowl, she strode toward the tomb.

This is Dina's tomb, Lillian thought. She pushed her hat deeper on her head and surveyed the wall. She had no tools that archeologists had but knew that Helmut and his soldiers would get them for her if she needed anything. She pushed her hands into her pockets. She decided to spend some time just viewing the exterior walls of the tomb in case there was something to be read or interpreted. She didn't know if there was. One thing was sure. She didn't want Dina to return to this world. She glanced back toward Helmut's tent. He stood by the tent's opening, staring at her. Lillian waved at him, gave a fake smile, and then turned her eyes to the wall.

Helmut should be pleased. I'm here. I've cooperated. That should be enough for today, she thought. *What a slimy, cruel man he is, threatening to kill me and making me watch my brother and Sawyer work like slaves.*

Lillian fumbled with the little piece of bone in her pocket. She wondered if it was important. It wasn't with the other skeletons, so the previous archeologists must have found it earlier. Another possibility was that the bone had been buried in the sand, and the tent was placed over it. Perhaps, it had nothing to do with this excavation area and the tomb.

She stared at the tomb's greyish exterior wall and let her eyes wander up and down the large structure. It is magnificent how the ancient workers crafted the huge blocks of limestones and fit them together so tight that you couldn't insert human hair between them. *It was surely built so tightly to keep a curse inside,* she thought. But was there more than one curse? She didn't know the answer to that.

Chapter 21

The Doorway's Curse

L illian saw some hieroglyphs carved around the doorway and moved toward it to see them better. She craned her neck holding her wide-brimmed hat with her hand, and mouthed the meaning of the carved images.

She had no reference book, so she couldn't be sure her translation was correct. Partly because the doorway's hieroglyphs were high up, she would have to climb up to see them more clearly.

Some symbols were quite similar, so she would have to look closer in case she made a mistake. It seemed that some hieroglyphs were also worn in the sand and time.

Frowning, Lillian painstakingly studied the characters and wished she had sheets of paper and a pen to write them down. It would be easier to do if she could write down what she thought each one meant.

Lillian knew that some characters had different meanings, and some, together with another hieroglyph, could mean a completely different thing, so she hesitated in her translation.

However, after a careful study, she was convinced that the carved message above the door stated a warning: "Whoever enters this tomb will release the evil onto the earth. Anubis protects the one whose remains are inside, and the buried one will rise when the first rays of sunshine hit the chamber."

She wasn't sure if her interpretation was correct. The chamber, for example, could be translated as the whole burial place or the tomb. She would have to study the images in more detail and closely. She could probably ask Helmut and his soldiers to build her a ladder or a temporary scaffold so she could climb up there and study the symbols better.

That's exactly what happened. Dina entered this world. Why didn't the previous archeologists care about the warning, or did they believe it was pure nonsense to scare away the graverobbers?

Lillian recalled that it had been morning when the Brits and the German archeologists opened the tomb. Just like the warning said, 'the buried one will arise when the sunshine hits the tomb.' The buried one was Dina, the daughter of Thutmose, the high priest.

She recalled Anubis, the god of the underworld, who had shown up in Berlin and threatened Dina. Dina had been afraid. She knew the god could take her away at that moment or let her finish her quest for the heart scarab. If it hadn't been for Sawyer, Jack, and Lillian, Dina could have succeeded in finding the scarab. Instead, they blew up the elevator and buried Dina's mortal body in the elevator. Dina had possessed the body of a young woman inside the blimp on their way to Berlin, so her body was mortal even though her evil spirit was supernatural. And now the Germans wanted to revive her again.

Lillian shook her head as she remembered how monstrous Dina had been: she killed anyone who stood between her and her goals. She didn't care for anyone. She would have been a cruel and violent ruler if she had succeeded.

She wondered if more hieroglyphs were not visible in her position. Now, she knew the curse was up there and recalled all that passed, but was there anything about reviving Dina again? She turned on her heels, walked to the closest soldier, and asked, "Could you ask Helmut if I could have ladders or a scaffold to climb up and examine the wall and the doorway closer? I also need some paper and a pen or pencils to draw the figures." She spoke in German so the soldier could understand her.

The soldier nodded. He glanced at his fellow soldier and said he would be back soon, then marched to Helmut's tent to deliver Lillian's message.

Lillian watched him go and then turned her eyes back to the tomb. Yes, she believed this tomb carried more mysteries than just one curse. The previous archeologists had released Dina, but there could be more. This tomb was built away from the Valley of the Kings, so perhaps there was another reason besides Dina inside it? The tomb was ready when Dina was sentenced to be buried alive.

Chapter 22

More Pressure

Lillian waited in the shade for a few hours as the workers built her a scaffold. She sat on one of the stones scattered around the excavation area. Her shade was the pyramid's shadow now as the sun had gone behind it.

While Sawyer was left to clean up the excavation site, his brother was with the scaffold builders. When he went by, Jack whispered, "Have you found something?"

"Yes, I think so. This tomb might have more secrets than just Dina. It was ready when she was killed, or so I believe, and thus, if this tomb was built before her death, then her curse was an addition, not the only one. Thutmose might have created more curses that we knew nothing about. We were never here before," Lillian replied, keeping an eye on the work supervisor, who seemed to notice Jack talking to her, so she added, "Go now. You'll be in trouble otherwise."

Jack nodded, moved away from his sister, picked up a log, and took it for the workers building the second level of the scaffold.

Lillian placed her hand over her eyes and searched for Roy Sawyer. She saw him carrying a pile of bones in a bucket to the edge of the excavation area where the Germans had dumped all the bones they had found. She wondered if it was worth going through them. There could be older bones, not just the previous workers and archeologists.

She wished she had learned more about Thutmose. She only knew that he was first the high priest and then advanced his position to the viceroy of the ancient kingdom of Egypt. He was wealthy, knowledgeable, and cunning, Lillian believed.

She looked at the wall where she had noticed the carving, which told the finalizing date when the tomb was finished. She knew that constructing a tomb this size usually took at least fifteen years, so construction had started long before Dina's death sentence. The date was 1290 BC, and his daughter Dina was killed in 1300 BC. Thus, the tomb was finished ten years before Dina was sentenced. Thutmose would have had plenty of time to create traps for graverobbers and curses. The question was, for what or whom had he originally planned this tomb? The more she thought about it, the more she believed that Dina's sentencing was unexpected, and Thutmose used this readymade tomb for her.

She glanced up as someone was approaching her. Helmut, of course, with his officer Karl Altman. She cursed in her mind. She didn't need extra pressure to read the hieroglyphs. She needed the scaffold to be ready to climb up and examine it more thoroughly.

The Germans stopped in front of her, and Helmut grabbed his white handkerchief again and wiped the sweat off his forehead. *He shouldn't be out here in this heat with his weight. He's going to have a heart attack soon,* Lillian thought, considering his red, sweaty face, but she wouldn't be sad if that happened. This man took them as prisoners in his camp and forced them to work for him. She turned her eyes from his face to his previously shiny black boots, which now had dust on them. *Too bad,* Lillian thought, your uniform is not immaculate now. *You'll have to ask your servant to clean them again.*

"Lillian," Helmut started, "we need you to pick up your pace. Heinrich Himmler, Reichsführer of the Schutzstaffel, has planned a quick visit to Africa to survey the Afrikakorps and then visit here. We want something to show him."

"When?" Lillian asked.

"In two days," Helmut replied.

Lillian raised her eyebrows. *Himmler is coming here! That's news.* She wished she could send a message to the Allies and let them know. They could capture him, and it would be a win for them. But she had no way to let the Allies know about that. She was stuck here with her brother and Sawyer.

"I'll work as fast as I can. As you see, your builders are done with the first level of the scaffold and building the next one. If you need results faster, you need more workers like your soldiers to help them. Otherwise, I can't help you. I'll wait down here in the shade until that structure is ready."

Helmut's hand lifted as if he was going to hit her, but then restrained himself and lowered his hand back to his side. He took Karl by the elbow, and they exchanged a few words further away so that Lillian didn't hear what they said, and then Helmut returned. "We'll work day and night from now on. No one sleeps until we have something to show to our Reichsführer."

Lillian looked stupefied. "How do you work in the nighttime? It's pitch dark. I can't see any hieroglyphs in the dark!"

"We'll get the spotlights. You'll see enough in their light to interpret the hieroglyphs and find something to show our Reichsführer," Helmut replied and turned on his heels, and marched back to his tent.

Karl went ahead and ordered everyone to work without rest until the scaffold was done. Lillian saw the grim faces. The soldiers knew that they would be up watching the workers. No rest for anyone. The heat was taking its toll on everyone, and now they were ordered to work double duty.

One of the local workers collapsed due to extreme heat and long work hours, but the soldiers kicked him and pulled him up. He stood there swaying as if he could not work, so the German soldiers beat him and left him on the ground. Karl Altmann announced, "He's an example for all of you. Work, and you'll be freed. If you don't work, you'll be punished. We have a deadline and will keep it regardless of how many of you will pass out or die."

Chapter 23

What's Written on the Wall?

For hours, Lillian waited for the scaffold to be ready. She had already dreamt of London's thick fog and rain and wished she'd never seen Egypt's dunes and palm trees.

A commotion interrupted her revelry. She craned her neck and saw that the last level of the scaffold was ready.

Sighing, she stood up and brushed the sand off her pants. *Time to go back to work.*

She took long strides to the end of the structure, where the ladders led to the next level and the following. The different levels allowed her to study the wall on the way up. She appreciated the design, probably due to the Germans' precision and skills rather than the workers' ideas.

When she ascended slowly, she studied the wall. It looked as if there were smaller hieroglyphs surrounding the bigger ones. She tilted her head as the images went around the bigger images as if someone had designed a larger text and then added something else around the first one. And again, she wished she had paper and pen or a camera with her, but she didn't have any of those. This would be a good time to take pictures or draw the images on paper and study them in a tent where it would be cooler. Now, she was forced to do everything standing while trying to hang on the scaffold's structure and take it all in at once. *Not the best way to thoroughly study the pyramid,* she thought.

As Lillian interpreted the images in her mind, she realized she was correct: The smaller images, when added to the bigger picture, revealed multiple curses. It first said that opening the tomb would release the demon, then the additional ones told another story. The first one warned about the dunes around the tomb being venomous. She wondered if that meant that the area was poisonous or if there were deadly insects. The images she saw surrounding the hieroglyphs reminded her of scorpions and black beetles. The next one warned that disturbing the inner peace of the tomb would release the wrath, whatever that meant. Lillian wondered if it was related to the traps that ancient Egyptians used to place inside the tombs. It was possible. She didn't believe that the first archeologists who opened the tomb had investigated it thoroughly. They encountered Dina when they opened the tomb so the rest would still be in pristine condition as it was left hundreds of years ago.

She furrowed her brow. If this was not meant to be Dina's burial place, who was the tomb's original owner?

Was it her father, the high priest? Then she remembered that Thutmose was buried at the Tombs of Nobles on the west side of the river Nile opposite the city of Luxor. She considered who could have afforded a burial place like this, and the only answer was the pharaoh himself or his heir. They had enough power and resources to build it, but why did they want it so far away from the Valley of the Kings? Unless they knew about the graverobbers and wanted this gravesite to be left alone. If it was further away, the thieves would most likely not wander this way and find it.

Now, she had two choices: tell Helmut and Karl what she had discovered, or not. This was nothing they could use to please their leaders.

Chapter 24

The Curse on the Wall

As Lillian stared at the hieroglyphs on the wall high up above the doorway, where the smaller images circled the bigger ones, she thought she saw a movement on the wall. The figures seemed to come alive and changed into snakes and scorpions. The snakes curled around the larger hieroglyphs, turned their heads to her, and opened their mouth, hissing at her.

She stepped back and grabbed the scaffold's rail; otherwise, she would have fallen to the sand and rocks. *The wall knows I'm reading it,* Lillian thought. *The snakes and the scorpions are getting ready to attack.*

Quickly, she descended the ladder to the previous level and studied the lower-level hieroglyphs. And the same thing happened, but this time they were the black beetles that scurried around the images on the wall. *Oh no, I have released something by reading the carvings,* she thought and continued downwards until she was back on the ground.

She looked around to find her brother and Sawyer. When she saw them standing by a pile of rocks, she quickly walked to them, ensuring that Helmut was not watching her. "Guys, I think we're in trouble. Reading the wall hieroglyphs started something evil. I think I unleashed another curse. The snakes, scorpions, and beetles on the wall came alive."

"That's impossible," Jack said, glancing at the tomb.

Sawyer did the same, and while they watched it, they noticed the wall surface was moving, as if something was alive there. "It's true. I see something moving there," Sawyer confirmed Lillian's words.

"What can we do?" Lillian asked, wringing her hands.

"We have to get the hell out of here," Sawyer replied. He glanced around to see where the nearest guard was. To his relief, the soldier was having a cigarette break and talking with the other guard. *They have a couple of minutes tops, he* thought grimly. "Let's leave now," he suggested.

The three of them ran away from the tomb towards the vehicles. They heard some angry voices behind them, but they didn't stop.

As Jack jumped inside the jeep and Sawyer pulled Lillian with him into the backseat, they heard the blood-curdling screams behind them. Curious, Lillian glanced back and saw the flow of snakes and scorpions covering the excavation area, killing the workers and heading to the tents.

Sawyer saw that too. He tapped Jack's shoulder and ordered, "Foot to the pedal now!"

Jack did as he was told, and the engine roared to life, and they drove forward. Lillian kept looking back to see what happened at the camp.

A figure came out of Helmut's tent, all covered in snakes and scorpions, screaming in pain. "Helmut," Lillian whispered as she stared at the gruesome sight.

The snakes and scorpions covered the body as it collapsed on the sand, then moved forward to the next one.

"Karl," Lillian muttered as she recognized their captor. His fate was not any better. The beetles covered him, digging under his skin, eating him alive. Soon, there was not much else but skeletons left on the ground. "That explains all the skeletons," Lillian mumbled.

Sawyer turned his eyes to her and asked, "What explains it?"

"I thought the area had more skeletons than there should be. You two piled hundreds of skeletons from the front of the tomb. This must have happened before. Someone else has tried to open the tomb, read the curse, and released the snakes, beetles, and scorpions," Lillian explained.

Sawyer nodded. "Yes, I thought there were a lot of skeletons too." He thought about it momentarily and then said, "If the tomb was accessed before, then the previous ones did not release Dina. They only read the curse on the wall. "

"Yes, I think some other archeologist group before Walther Wolfe and Sir Michael Merriweather discovered this grave but didn't have time to report it because of the curse on the wall," Lillian replied.

"So many skeletons." Jack sighed. "I wish we had never met Dina and found this tomb."

Sawyer said, "Keep your eyes on the road. Not all the Germans were at the camp. I saw three vehicles leaving for Cairo earlier, so they will be back."

"The curse only works when you are near the tomb," Lillian commented, "Because none of the bugs and snakes came after us." She glanced back to make sure she was right. Sighing, she saw no signs of snakes or scorpions.

"That's likely why the Germans were alive when we arrived. They had not read the tomb wall and released the curse yet," Sawyer said.

"Where should we go?" Jack asked, trying to keep a steady pace driving up and down the dunes.

"Go back to the camp," Lillian said. "I don't believe they will look for us there."

"Is there something you're looking for?" Jack asked.

"I'm not sure." Lillian frowned. "I know the Germans took most of the materials we had gathered, but perhaps they left something behind." She swirled the little bone in her pocket and pulled it out. "This one was not by the tent. Why was it at the camp? It must mean something."

"Or nothing." Jack kept his eyes on the dunes and the horizon, making sure they were heading in the right direction. "I agree that we should not go to our hotel in Cairo now. That's where the Germans will look for us first."

Chapter 25

Dina

Dina followed the events folding in the living world. She was unhappy that Aper's bone had not entered the tomb and wondered what her father, Thutmose, had done. She knew it was built before she was sentenced, and she had thought it was meant for him, but his tomb was found in the Tombs of Nobles, where all the high-ranking officials were buried. So, who was this tomb for? She had only one answer: the pharaoh himself. However, one thing puzzled her with that conclusion: Why did Pharaoh Akhenaten have his tomb built so far away from the Valley of the Kings? The valley was the place for the rulers.

Unless he had planned to hide something valuable in this tomb, and it was never supposed to be a burial tomb. That would explain the extra curses. Those were done even before Dina was buried alive there. Her father had never explained the reason for its construction. She had always suspected it was a burial tomb, but it could have been a treasure tomb.

Dina had wished to meet her father in the underworld, but because she was cursed, she was not allowed to approach the uncursed ones. She had to stay apart until her curse was broken, or she had returned and fulfilled her destiny in the world above. So, she was in a limbo state, waiting for the right moment. She wondered what area was reserved for slaves like Aper, who had done nothing evil on earth but were not buried correctly. She was sure it was some sort of indeterminate area in the world of the dead, but he was not where she was.

Dina wondered if she could use the tomb's secrets to lure the archeologist woman and her brother there. She would be interested in finding treasure inside the tomb. Although Dina was not sure the tomb had any treasures buried, she hoped there were. She didn't know if the tomb was used before she was buried there. However, she didn't have to know that she only needed to get Lillian to take the bone inside there, and thus, Aper would be allowed to rest in peace.

She had left, and the German soldiers were dead, so the tomb was empty. If only she could find out what the curse was that her father had cast on the tomb's walls... She had no idea what it was but knew her father had written down all his curses and spells. What if Dina could find another way to the tomb, and thus, Lillian and her companions could avoid the outer wall's curse? The builders always had a secret entranceway they used when they finished the tomb. Her father would not have built a tomb without one.

Dina was sure that Lilian would be glad to explore the tomb because she would gain more authority in the archeologist world and thus become famous. She would have to find a way to communicate with her. She'd used the bat before. Perhaps, she could do that again, but this time, she'd have to communicate with Lillian and explain what she wanted and what Lillian would get in exchange for it.

She waited until Anubis was occupied with new souls entering the underworld and snuck out. She took the form of the large bat again. She headed to Cairo first but couldn't find Lillian and her brother there, so she went to the camps. And there they were!

Chapter 26

At the Camp Again

T he luminous moon was in the indigo night sky with bright stars. Dina had chosen the nighttime to enter the world of the living because the barrier was thinner at that time of day than at any other time.

In the form of a large bat, she flew toward the camp of Germans. She noted the jeep parked near the biggest tent and assumed it was the same one Lillian and her companions had taken.

Circling the tent, she tried to see inside. Her vision was excellent, but the fabric was closed on all the sides of the tent; thus, she had to figure out a way to enter the tent or get Lillian to come out.

She sat on top of the hood of the Jeep and started shrieking loudly. After a while, someone opened the tent, and Dina saw Sawyer looking outside. He saw the bat and cursed. "It's the bat again!"

The bat didn't attack or fly toward him this time but sat still as if waiting for something.

Lillian peeked behind him. "If that's Dina, then let her take the initiative. I want to know what she wants from us."

Dina heard that. She flapped her wings once but didn't fly away.

Lillian stared at her curiously. "Flap once if you're Dina."

The bat listened and obeyed. *One flap. Yes, I'm Dina.*

"She's Dina! That's why she was after us. How do we get her to tell us what she wants?" Lillian strode toward the vehicle and stopped a few feet away from the bat. They stared at each other. Both Jack and Sawyer followed her.

"If she can communicate with either shrieks or flapping her wings, then ask her simple yes or no questions," Jack commented, glaring at the ugly bat.

"Do you want something from us?" Lillian asked.

One flap. Yes.

"Is it something that we have?" Sawyer asked.

One flap. Yes.

"Is it something that we can do?" Jack asked.

One wing flap again.

"If it is something we have and also something we can do, then how do we find out what it is?" Lillian furrowed her brows.

"Perhaps, she could come inside the tent and point hieroglyphs," Jack suggested. "She knows the ancient language and hieroglyphs, so that's the best way to communicate."

The bat agreed, and thus, Dina took off and flew inside the tent. The others followed her there.

Lillian grabbed a book with hieroglyphs and their explanations. She opened it on the table. The bat sat in the corner of the table, then shrieked when she saw an image of a tomb. "Your visit has something to do with the tomb," Lillian suggested.

The bat flapped her wing once.

"Isn't this weird?" Sawyer said. "We're trying to figure out why Dina is in the form of a bat when we were the ones she forced to help her the last time, and then we stopped her with the explosion in the elevator. Why are we doing this questioning? We could just chase her away." He waved his arms at the bat. "Shoo!"

The bat moved a bit but didn't leave.

"There must be a reason why she came back," Lillian said, glancing at Sawyer. "Let's find out."

She turned the pages of the old hieroglyph book, but the bat didn't seem interested in any images. "This is not working. Let's try another book," Lillian said, grabbing the book with images of the pyramids.

The bat got more agitated when she saw the pyramids. She pointed at them and the images of the excavation of Tutankhamon's tomb. "It's the tomb." Lillian stared at the bat. "You want us to go back to the tomb." One flap of a wing again.

"Why? What's in it for me or you?" Lillian asked.

The bat walked closer and then pointed at her pocket where the bone was. Lillian pulled it out. "This bone. It means something to you, doesn't it?"

The bat flapped her wing again.

"You want this bone to go back to the excavation area?" Lillian asked.

Two flaps. No, not there.

"Inside the tomb, then?" Lillian kept questioning.

One flap.

"We can't go inside. The tomb is cursed," Jack commented.

Two flaps.

"You're saying we can go inside the tomb without being killed?" Jack's eyes veered from the bat to Lillian's eyes.

One flap.

"You know of a secret entrance to the tomb," Lillian said.

The bat didn't move her wings.

"You believe there is a secret entrance, but you don't know where," Lillian said, and the bat flapped her wings once again.

"If we use the hidden entryway, then we won't die from the curse," Sawyer said, staring at the bat.

One flap of wings.

"So, let me get this straight: you want me to take this bone inside the tomb, and if we do that, you'll find us the other entrance where we won't get killed?" Lillian asked.

One flap. The bat turned its mysterious eyes toward Sawyer and then back to Lillian and Jack.

"I don't see why we should go back. That tomb is cursed. Why would we want to enter that place?" Sawyer said.

"It could be worth it if there are treasures or maps of ancient Egypt," Lillian replied. The bat flapped her wings once.

Sawyer glared at the bat. "You were not our friend last time when we met you. Why would you help us now?"

The bat pointed with her wing to the bone Lillian was holding.

"That piece of bone means something to you. That's why you're here," Lillian deduced. She shrugged. "I can go to the tomb. I'm not afraid of curses. Besides, if Dina goes with us, the curses might not awaken." She looked at her companions, and they both appeared stern.

But after giving it some thought, they both nodded in agreement. "Okay, we can go there, but we'll go together. All of us, including Dina the bat. We won't let you go alone," Sawyer warned.

Venomous Dunes

The moon and the stars were the only witnesses as Lillian, Jack, and Sawyer left with the huge bat towards the excavation camp and the tomb again.

The cool night air would have been refreshing after the hot sunny day though the wind picked up, and the sand stung like bees on their skin as they walked towards the jeep and sat inside the vehicle.

Jack started the engine and drove behind the huge bat, who, from time to time, circled the car making sure they were following, and then flew ahead. Jack glanced at Sawyer, who sat next to him. "Are you sure this is wise? The snakes and the scorpions could kill us if Dina does not know where the secret entrance is."

Sawyer shook his head. "I don't know about this. She came to us asking for a favor, or so it seems. I don't trust her any more than I did the last time."

"We don't know if she's working with Anubis or against him," Lillian said behind them from the back seat.

"That does not make me feel any better," Jack grumbled but kept driving.

They saw the bat in the jeep's headlights and followed her. The bat flew higher, and they could see her shadow cast on the dunes as Dina headed directly to the tomb.

The wind blew more sand across the previous tracks. If anyone was looking for them, they wouldn't find the tracks.

When they were within sight of the excavation area and the tomb, Jack stopped the vehicle and left the headlights on so that they could see the area. He wished he had not done that.

The long, dark form of the tomb loomed ahead.

Sawyer said, "Don't go closer. I have a bad feeling about it. Remember how the Germans died? The snakes and the scorpions and other bugs."

"Yes, I remember. I'll stop here." Jack stopped the engine, picked up the flashlight, and shone it toward the area ahead.

Lillian swallowed and whimpered, "Look at the bodies of the German soldiers. They are all dead; some bodies have no flesh left, just skeletons."

And just as she said it, the nearest part of the tomb's shadow, which defined itself by the thinnest light of the moon that reached that place, moved.

"Point over there. I thought I saw something moving near the tomb's shadow," Sawyer said to Jack, who did as he was asked.

He saw the deadly snakes slithering and the scorpions crawling in the sand near the tomb. The curse had set them free, and now they were waiting for more visitors.

"There's no way we can get in without getting bitten or stung," Sawyer said as he watched the venomous dunes ahead. The snakes and the scorpions seemed to know that visitors were close by as they gathered at the edge of the excavation area, but they didn't crawl any further. Raised no more than a few inches, the snakes hovered their heads up and stared in the jeep's direction with their mouths open, flicking their forked tongues and showing their teeth. The scorpions had their deadly tails up and scurried along the excavation area's edge.

"They all stopped, and now they are waiting for us if we go ahead," Sawyer commented as he stared at the critters and the snakes on the dunes.

"We can't get past that venomous area unless Dina finds the secret entrance," Lillian replied, adding, "It's not unheard of that the builders had an additional entryway to the tombs. They had to deliver items inside and also make sure that the tomb was ready for its use. Besides, they didn't want to walk inside the tomb using the obvious entrance because of the curses placed there. Where is Dina?" Lillian glanced up. She didn't see the bat anywhere.

The guys looked around, searching the sky, but they couldn't see her either.

"Did she leave us? Is this a trap?" Sawyer asked, furrowing his brows and raising in his seat. He scanned the area around them, but couldn't see further because the night was dark.

Chapter 28

The Secret Entrance to the Tomb

Dina had flown ahead when the jeep stopped before Jack took out his flashlight. As she was the color of an onyx-grey cloud, it was easy for her to be invisible against the dark sky. Her wingspan was about five feet, so she was like a huge kite flying across the sky, casting a giant shadow underneath her on the dunes. She viewed the tomb from all sides and then flew further away, looking for signs of another entrance. Then she saw a formation of stones. It wasn't a tomb but it was close enough to be the secret entrance. It was in the opposite direction from the excavation area on the front side, where the main entrance to the tomb was.

Dina thought hiding the secret path from the main view made sense. She circled the stones and was more certain now that this was the right place. The stones looked old but similar to the tomb's stones made of limestone, like the pyramids in the Valley of the Kings. She took another round around the area and saw no pyramids nearby. Her tomb was the only one near these stones. *This has to be it,* she thought and flew back to find Lillian and her companions.

Lillian cradled the little bone in the palm of her hand. *What is so special about this bone? It must belong to someone Dina loved. It can't be her father's, but could it be the reason she died: her slave lover? The slave was tortured and killed before she was buried alive in the tomb.* She sighed wearily, looked at Jack and Sawyer, and asked, "What if this bone belonged to the man she loved, the slave?"

"It's possible," Jack replied, glancing back. "She might want to reunite with him in the underworld. That would make this effort to find the secret entrance worthwhile to her."

"Yes, we only know that her discretion was to love a lowly slave when she was supposed to save herself for the gods of ancient Egypt, and thus the pharaoh sentenced both of them to die," Lillian replied. "As you said, it would make sense."

"Where did that horrific bat fly?" Sawyer asked crankily. "I don't see her anywhere. I'm starting to doubt her intentions."

At first, Lillian heard a shriek. She jackknifed into a sitting position and surveyed the sky. "She's nearby," she told Jack and Sawyer. From the darkness, the bat emerged, her large wings open, revealing its snouted face and pointy ears. She looked like an evil incarnated in all of her grotesqueness, but all Lillian could focus on were those sharp teeth as she opened her mouth and shrieked.

Lillian wasn't sure if she should duck or sit still. The bat looked ferocious. She tried to keep her racing heart calm and not move. "Did you find it?"

Dina, the bat, shrieked, turned around, flew past the jeep, and circled toward the back of the tomb. She looked eager to show them something.

"Let's go! Don't lose her," Lillian said, tapping Jack on the shoulder. Quickly Jack started the car and drove after the enormous bat, avoiding going too close to the excavation area and the waiting snakes and scorpions. The headlights bounced ahead from the dunes as Jack tried to follow the bat's route.

The snakes saw their victims move, and they slithered into action. The scorpions scurried ahead, following an invisible line that the curse had made that stopped them from crossing the line and attacking the jeep. Thus, they followed, hoping they would reach the jeep and its passengers if they stepped even one foot over the curse line and intruded on the peace of the tomb like the Germans had.

The wind blew Lillian's hair on her face, and she couldn't see much. She had to hold tight on the side of the car to avoid falling off the jeep when Jack swerved and drove up and down the dunes trying to follow the bat. Jack had decided to keep the bat in sight so she couldn't disappear again from them.

Chapter 29

The Underground Path

D ina swooped down and sat down on the stones she had found. The jeep followed her and parked near the formation.

"The bat is there," Jack commented. "Could that be the secret entrance?"

"It's possible." Roy Sawyer glanced back towards the tomb and saw that the scorpions and snakes crawled around it, but they didn't come where these stones were this far. "I think we are safe to stop here. It looks like the critters and the snakes can't approach us."

Jack parked the jeep, and they all climbed out. Dina flapped her wings but didn't leave the stones. She had to make sure this was the secret entrance.

Lillian circled the stone formation and said, "Let's grab the shovels from the trunk. We need to dig here. I can't see if this is an entrance or not."

They pushed hard for a couple of hours in the moonlight. Exhaustion was beginning to take a toll when they finally cleared enough sand from around the stones that Lillian could see a large limestone blocking the entrance. "We have to move that away to see where it leads," she said tiredly.

They grabbed bottles of water from the trunk of the Jeep and then went back to work. Both Sawyer and Jack had to use all their muscles to push away the large stone, and when it finally rolled away, it revealed an opening. Lillian peaked inside. It was blacker than a moonless night.

Dina looked restless, turning her head up into the sky.

Lillian noticed it and said, "You can go now. I believe we have found the entrance to the tomb. I will place the bone inside your tomb."

Dina shrieked once, then zoomed upward to the dark sky and flew away, disappearing into the night. She had to return to the underworld before Anubis missed her. She flew fast as she knew the nighttime was short, and soon it would be dawn. She couldn't stay in this world past sunrise. Already the lighter blue color tinged the horizon.

The dank and dark path beyond the stone they pushed away was made of stone like the tomb was built so the sand would not enter it. The tunnel led toward Dina's tomb. It had been sealed centuries ago by the last of the tomb workers. Sawyer went to grab the flashlights to illuminate the man's size pathway. The silence in the tunnel made Lillian, Jack, and Sawyer feel like intruders trespassing on a gravesite. They proceeded slowly inside the tunnel, and soon they entered a large room with paintings of Anubis with pharaohs and their servants on the walls.

What their eyes beheld was more stunning than anything they had ever believed to see. Jack stepped backward, nearly bumping into Lillian and Sawyer, who stumbled briefly and then caught their balance. Before them was an entire wall filled with maps and papyrus scrolls; beneath the shelves were piles of golden coins, statues, and jewels.

"This was a treasure chamber!" Lillian sighed, looking around, admiring the artwork on the walls and the golden statues of the gods on the floor.

"Let's start hauling these away," Jack said practically. As he stepped forward, he saw another tunnel leading almost parallel to the one they had entered this room. "I wonder where that leads?"

Lillian stood beside him, saying, "It could be another entrance to this treasure chamber."

Sawyer had strolled towards the piles of gold coins and statues, and when he picked up one of the statues, they heard a loud rumbling.

"Oh no!" Lillian glanced back and saw what Sawyer had done. "It's a trap! We have to leave!" She quickly dropped the piece of bone on the ground inside the tomb as she had promised Dina.

Lillian rushed toward the tunnel where they had come from with Sawyer, whereas Jack was too slow, and he decided to grab some maps and papyruses, stuffed them inside his shirt, and ran to the other tunnel.

This was the first time they were separated, Jack thought as he ran through the new tunnel, his flashlight's beam bouncing ahead of him. He saw the stone blocking his entrance and pushed it away by leaning on it and using his leg muscles. At first, the stone didn't move much, but gradually, it started rolling aside. Luckily, that entry was higher on the ground, and the dunes had not covered it with sand. However, it had taken him some time to get out of the tunnel, and the sandstorm had started. He couldn't see much of anything with the howling wind. He walked ahead, and soon he arrived near the area where they had parked the vehicle but didn't see Lillian and Sawyer.

Where are they? Jack wondered about it as he sat down. He covered his mouth with a scarf and crouched next to the vehicle so that it would give him some shelter. The sandstorm lasted hours. When the wind finally calmed down, Jack saw it was already midday. He stood up, brushed his clothes from the sand, and grabbed a water bottle from the trunk.

I have to find Lillian and Sawyer. He tried to call their names, but there was no reply.

Chapter 30

Aper's Path in the Afterlife

The Duat and the spirit's journey in the afterlife

W hile the deceased Egyptians who had undergone the traditional mummification process found their way to Duat, the realm of the afterlife, to be presented before Osiris, the king of the netherworld, Aper's journey had deviated from this expected trajectory. As a slave of low societal standing and one condemned to death by the pharaoh, he had been denied this customary passage. Yet, an unexpected opportunity had arisen with Lillian placing his bones within Dina's burial site, nestled within her tomb.

In the underworld, Anubis guarded the entrance to the underworld. The god had the scales of justice on his one hand, to weigh their heart in the scale against the feather of the goddess Ma'at. If the heart passed the test, the recently deceased would be given the right to enter the Fields of Rushes, the heavenly view of life on earth.

Conversely, if the heart was heavy with sins and bad deeds, it would be given to Ammut, the Devourer.

Dina flew past Anubis as he was busy with his scales. Anubis glanced around as he thought someone passed him but didn't notice Dina.

Dina emerged behind the god, then stood there waiting for her old lover to appear. She believed Lillian's word that the piece of Aper's bone would be taken into the tomb. She hoped the humans had succeeded in the task.

Soon after, she saw the familiar figure approaching the gate.

Anubis glanced at him and then behind him, saw Dina waiting for Aper.

"You made it happen," Anubis growled at Dina.

Dina looked at him innocently. "What do you mean?" she replied flippantly.

"Aper is at the gate." Anubis turned his jackal head toward the newly arrived man.

He took his heart and weighed it. It was not heavy. His crimes were not severe in the world of the living, so he was allowed to pass.

Dina threw her arms around his neck when he walked through the gate. "Aper! Finally, you're here." Aper took her in his arms, and they kissed each other fiercely.

Their reunion didn't last long, as Anubis interrupted them. "Aper, you can proceed to the Fields of Rushes. You'll be a free man there." Then Anubis faced Dina and said, "You will stay here in limbo because you still have not fulfilled your task, and your father cursed you in that tomb."

Dina's arms fell, and she stared at Anubis, not believing what she had just heard. "You can't be serious."

Aper lowered his arms and stood still. Seeing Dina had been an unexpected pleasure but leaving her this soon was disappointing. But he couldn't argue against Anubis. He knew that.

Anubis gestured to Aper to go, and he had no choice but to proceed to the heavenly fields, whereas Dina stood still, staring after him. She turned to Anubis and asked, "When is my turn to pass the gate and go there?"

"When the curse is broken, or you fulfill what your father demanded: revenge in the world of the living," Anubis replied, staring at Dina with his sharp jackal eyes.

Dina stomped her foot on the ground. "No, no! This can't be happening! I want to be with Aper." She turned her fiery eyes on Anubis and asked, "Where is my father,

Thutmose? I want him to undo the curse. I don't want to go back to the world of the living. I want to be with Aper."

"Your father passed these gates centuries ago. He's in the Fields of Rushes and spends his afterlife in a comfortable palace," Anubis replied. "He can't undo the curse because he's not in the world of the living. Only a living person can break the curse, or you have to return to that world again someday. Until that happens, you're stuck in limbo." Anubis glared at Dina and then returned to his place by the gates of the underworld.

"But... but how long do I stay here?" Dina asked desperately, wringing her hands.

"I don't know. It depends on the world of the living and when you can re-enter there. It's not today and not tomorrow," Anubis replied calmly. He gestured for another recently passed soul to come forward and continued weighing the hearts.

Sighing, Dina turned and glanced behind the barrier of the heavenly fields. She would not see Aper more today or tomorrow.

Chapter 31

What Happened to Our Adventurers?

While Jack was still struggling to get out of the tomb, an extremely strong sandstorm hit. Lillian and Sawyer couldn't see anything as the wind with the sand stung their faces. They curled near the entrance and tried to stay in the cover.

Their wish was not granted.

The gold statue had triggered a trap, and the tunnel started collapsing and caving. Running as fast as they could, Sawyer pulled Lillian after him while the sand beneath them had turned into quicksand with no solid stone floor.

Sawyer cursed as he noticed it and kept running, and he jumped outside of the entrance the minute everything behind him turned into a swirl of sand. He held Lillian's hand in his and pulled her to safer ground. They stared at the bottomless sand pit where the entrance had been. Sighing in relief, they looked at each other. At least they were safe now.

"We have to go. We can't stay here," Sawyer yelled at Lillian. It was hard to hear anything as the wind howled loudly.

Sawyer grabbed Lillian by the hand and pulled her with him as he walked slowly against the howling wind. He tugged down his desert scarf to cover his face and hoped the storm would not last for hours. Lillian did the same with her scarf.

Hoping to find their jeep, he pulled Lillian with him. However, he couldn't see where they were going as they ran away from the entrance that sank into the desert.

Sawyer tried to look around in the storm, but it was impossible. He thought they'd gone in the same direction, but he didn't see Jack anywhere.

He saw a couple of camels lying on the ground and rushed there. "We'll stay with these camels. They will give us some protection," he said to Lillian and pulled her next to him.

"Whose camels are these?" Lillian asked.

"I don't know. The Germans or their local workers probably had them in the camp," Sawyer replied. They crouched together, leaning against the camels and trying to be as small as possible so that the storm's force would not hit them so hard.

Sawyer saw a blanket on top of the camel's satchel bag and pulled it out to cover their bodies with it as they waited for the wind to calm down.

It took a long time before the wind stilled and the storm passed. When it had, Sawyer pushed the blanket away and looked around. Everything looked different. He saw no familiar landmarks.

Lillian kneeled next to him, looking quizzical. "Where are we?"

"I don't know." Sawyer stood up and walked a bit further, trying to see Jack or the tomb, but he didn't see either one. He shook his head as he returned to Lillian. "I don't see Jack."

Lillian's face turned worried, and Sawyer quickly added, "He's not dead. He had plenty of time to run past that other entrance. I'm sure he's fine. Most likely, he found the jeep and is now looking for us."

"We have to stay together," Lillian said. "We don't have any water or food. If we don't find him, then we'll be in trouble. We can't survive in this desert for a long time."

"I know that." Sawyer looked again at the horizon but didn't see anyone moving in any direction.

Meanwhile, Jack tried to get the jeep started. It had got some sand inside its engine, and he had to take some time to fix the problem, which he luckily managed to do. He had water in the trunk, and while drinking it, he glanced at the papyruses he had grabbed. They talked about the last war, the female warrior, and the lost treasure. *Interesting,* he thought. *Lillian will be glad to see these.*

As Jack couldn't find Lillian and Sawyer, he returned to Cairo and got more food and water. *Lillian and Sawyer will need them,* he thought as he started the car and drove away.

So, their paths were separated, but all had survived the venomous dunes.

Will Jack find his sister and Roy Sawyer? Find out and read

The Lost Oasis of Love!

The Next Books
In The Series

ARLA JONES
the
lost
Oasis
OF LOVE

ARLA JONES
MUMMY
RETURNS
She will rule the living and the dead

Also By

Fathers and Sons

Bugs on Vella

Black Dust

The Facility

The Ashburn -series:

On Death's Door

Finders Keepers

The Cupid and the Elf -series:

Love Trap

Naughty Elf

The Cursed series:

The Cursed Banshee

The Iguana series:

The Attack of the Iguana

My book links: https://linktr.ee/authorarlajones

Ongoing projects: https://beacons.ai/arlajonesbooks

preorders: https://linktr.ee/preordersajbooks

https://www.pinterest.com/authorarlajones/

Facebook: https://www.facebook.com/authorarlajones

www.tiktok.com/@jonesesbooks

Instagram: https://www.instagram.com/authorarlajones/

My author page: https://authorarlajones.wordpress.com/